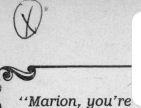

"Marion, you're

"My name is Miss Mathieson, and you, sir, are a sheep. Follow the herd, and have nothing to do with such untamed wildlife as I. I will not be dictated to by—"

A blaze of frustration flared over Kestrel's hawkish features. He less resembled a sheep than a wolf as he pulled me into his arms. From there it flamed to a primitive battle, to see which of us could outdo the other in ardor. I wasn't going to be bested in anything by this man, including passion.

As his arms crushed me mercilessly against his chest, I wrapped mine around his waist and squeezed till he was gasping. I responded from the top of my head to the ends of my toes. I hadn't been so exhilarated since that night I was chased down a mountain by a band of Arabs.

Also by Joan Smith
Published by Fawcett Books:

BABE

AURORA

LACE FOR MILADY

VALERIE

THE BLUE DIAMOND

REPRISE

WILES OF A STRANGER

LOVER'S VOWS

RELUCTANT BRIDE

LADY MADELINE'S FOLLY

LOVE BADE ME WELCOME

MIDNIGHT MASQUERADE

ROYAL REVELS

THE DEVIOUS DUCHESS

TRUE LADY

BATH BELLES

STRANGE CAPERS

A COUNTRY WOOING

LOVE'S HARBINGER

LETTERS TO A LADY

COUNTRY FLIRT

LARCENOUS LADY

MEMOIRS OF A HOYDEN

Joan Smith

FAWCETT CREST • NEW YORK

A Fawcett Crest Book
Published by Ballantine Books
Copyright © 1988 by Joan Smith

ISBN 0-449-21329-3

Manufactured in the United States of America

First Edition: May 1988

Chapter One

The lengthening shadows of twilight made reading difficult in the coach, so I closed up my leather lap case and set it on the floor at my feet. As we had been joggling along in the coach for nearly three hours, I estimated we must be some twenty miles east of London, with still thirty to go before we reached Canterbury. My lecture was not to be delivered till the next evening, however, so I would stop over at Chatham for a good night's sleep and to practice my delivery on Mr. Kidd, my secretary cum traveling companion cum friend, and occasionally ad hoc nephew, if my host proved a trifle high in the instep.

These artificial constraints are vexing after my travels abroad. Are the English so lecher-minded they can't credit a single lady and gentleman might travel together without being lovers—especially when the lady is past thirty, the gentleman a decade younger? I have traveled half the world, going from Portsmouth to Gilbraltar on a warship, and very comfortable it was, too. I took a frigate from Gilbraltar to Zanta, in the Ionian Sea, and enjoyed the company of the commander-in-chief of the islands. Thence by felucca to the Gulf of Corinth, and by a wretched Greek polacca to see the Hellespont, famed for having been swum by Leander to see his Hero, and by Byron to give himself something else to

1

brag about. Ronald Kidd swam it, too, but he didn't sit down and write a poem to commemorate the event. To cut short my itinerary, I have been across the Syrian desert and seen the ruins of Zenobia's legendary town, Palmyra. Prior to our arrival, only three European men had seen the sight, and one of them was beaten and robbed. I made most of my travels in the company of raffish Arab males, without losing either my dignity or my virginity. A lady may be unconventional without being fast. I have heard myself called odd, headstrong, hurly-burly, and egocentric, but never fast, till I returned to England to have my memoirs published.

It was Mr. Oates, my publisher, who came up with the notion that a circuit of lectures would increase sales. I believe I can say without courting immodesty that the initial talks in London went over very well. The hall was filled to the doors all three nights, and no less a luminary than Thomas Moore came to speak to me afterward. He has a string of oriental tales in verse he wished to discuss, but time prevented my looking at it on that occasion.

The carriage hit a bump, jogging me back to the present. If I remained long in England, I would certainly have to set up a carriage and team. It wasn't the expense that deterred me, but the uncertain duration of my stay. The East beckoned me back. I particularly missed the starry dusk of Constantinople, with the Bosphorus glowing like liquid fire as the sun set. Greece, too, was only passed through. April was supposed to be the best of England's weather, but the sky above us at that moment was leaden gray, and had been for three days. The sun, on those odd moments when it was visible at all, was only a pale white disk showing shyly behind clouds. With nothing pleasant to see beyond the carriage, I cast an eye around at my companions.

A certain Mr. Wideman, a traveling salesman in what he called the "toy and trinket" line, had been bending

2

Mr. Kidd's ear mercilessly. What he purveyed were glass beads for servants and tin chains and watch fobs for clerks who in all probability had no watch to attach to them, but would like the respectability of a chain to hint at one. He had opened his case and revealed these garish trinkets for our delectation as soon as the carriage left the coaching office. His importunings reminded me of the street Arabs, though in appearance he could hardly be less similar. He was fat and red-faced, whereas they were cadaverously thin and brown-skinned, their poor, emaciated bodies wrapped in swaddling rags.

He caught my eye and pushed a set of red glass beads at me. "Ruby glass," he assured me. "A great bargain at half a crown. They are a new item, hot from London, Miss Mathieson. See the dainty clasp, with a bit of red glass set into it, like a genuine jewel."

"Very pretty," I smiled, and turned aside hastily, before he dunned me to buy one.

The other occupant of the coach was a cleric. When he noticed I had closed my lap case, he turned a sanctimonious eye on me and introduced himself. "Reverend Cooke, from Canterbury," he smiled. He was a closer match to the Arab street peddlers, insofar as build went. He was one of those skeletal gentlemen who emanated cold piety. For all that, I had noticed he wasn't reading the copy of Dr. Donne's *Devotions and Sermons* he held in his lap, but was using it to conceal some drawings of females en dishabille. I don't mean to say the drawings were lecherous, but only suggestive. I got a peek when the carriage lurched around a narrow corner.

This would no doubt have shocked some provincial ladies. I am immune to that sort of shock after my travels. It is all a matter of custom. In Damascus a lady risks her life if she shows her face to the world, whereas the Druse women in the mountains of Lebanon expose their faces and half their breasts. Men are the same the world over—they decree that some part of the female anatomy must be kept hidden, and spend the rest of their lives trying to get a glimpse of it. It all has to do with trying to make us poor women mysterious and therefore desirable. I refuse to find anything disgusting in the attraction between the sexes. There is something undignified if not downright ridiculous in the way procreation has been arranged, but it is not disgusting. It is the prudery that I despise most. Reverend Cooke began some boring discussion of John Donne's sermons, and I revised my opinion. Hypocrisy is most despicable. And for all his pictures, Cooke had the temerity to suggest that I was ''daring'' to travel without a female companion! I knew what he meant by that euphemism. Mr. Kidd became my nephew, and the reverend's eyebrows returned to their normal level.

The carriage lurched to a stop, causing us all to wonder what was amiss, for the countryside showed nothing in the way of a village or even a coaching house. Mr. Wideman opened the door and soon reported what was afoot. ''Some young lad has broken the axle of his curricle and wants a lift to Chatham with us,'' he announced.

The ''young lad'' suddenly came into view, speaking to his groom, and I looked with interest. ''Young'' is entirely a relative word. A gentleman of thirty-two, for instance, is ''young,'' whereas a lady such as myself of that age who is still single is considered pretty ancient. The gentleman in question appeared to be in his mid-thirties—whether that is old or young you may judge for yourself. As to the rest of it, I shall judge for you that he was handsome. You must bear in mind, however, that I have a certain fondness for swarthy gentlemen. The foolish moth part of me is attracted to that hint of the foreign. This one's face was well weathered, but his features were pure Anglo-Saxon. His eyes, a pearly gray color, looked quite striking, set in that tanned face. The hair that showed beneath his curled beaver was black as jet. He looked a sort of cross between Byron and a proud desert sheikh, with his chiseled nose and concrete jaw. His well-tailored jacket and general air of breeding, if you can overlook a few accomplished oaths, put him in the bracket of gentleman. A shiny yellow curricle and perfectly matched pair of grays harnessed to it spoke of wealth. His general build and posture suggested an interest in athletic activities—broad shoulder, tapering to a slim waist. Well-muscled legs filled a pair of elegant tan trousers, terminating in shining Hessians. One doesn't see many gentlemen so well built in the Orient, where men tend to be smaller in stature. Indeed, were I to take a trick from Reverend Cooke and carry a set of pictures hidden in my lap case, the gentleman beyond the window would make a fine model, unless his shoulders were all padding.

He soon passed beyond sight. The carriage lurched again as he clambered atop with John Groom, and we were off. Before we had gone half a mile, the rain that had been threatening all day began slanting down. I thought this might drive our new passenger into the coach, where his company would have been appreciated, but it was no such a thing. He had carried a drab driving coat with him, which no doubt was well turned up around his chin by now, for the rain was coming down quite hard. Another half mile passed, and as the sun had set, I closed my eyes and soon nodded off to sleep.

To think, I nearly slept through the most interesting occurrence since returning to England! And that despite a pistol shot, which still echoed in my ears. Mr. Kidd, knowing my nature, jostled my arm. "Marion," he said, "didn't you hear it? You won't want to miss this!"

I opened my eyes and blinked at Ronald. He is slender, pale, and scholarly, which is not to say he is a man milliner. He has proven a very capable friend and co-hort. "What is it?" I asked, coming to attention.

"We're being held up by highwaymen," he grinned. "What excellent timing!"

It is well no one overheard his strange remark. The cleric and Mr. Wideman were speaking together in shocked whispers, discussing where it was best to hide their money. It is clear the reason for the "excellent timing" requires an explanation. In fact, I might as well get a whole lump of necessary explanation over with at once, though I am sorry it must delay a description of our encounter with the highwaymen.

It must have occurred to you before now that a young lady's traveling abroad more or less unattended was strange. If I am strange, so be it. I am at least not lily-livered enough to accept a life of tedium. I am the only daughter of the late Captain Mathieson, who was with Wellesley in the Peninsula. I followed the drum with Papa, which gave me a taste for travel. When my father was killed early in the campaign, I was sent home to Sussex, where I languished for a year with my aunt. Being in deep mourning, I seldom went out. The long hours were beguiled relating my adventures to my cousins and their neighbors. They were quite simply fascinated by the unusual experiences I had enjoyed.

"It ought to be put into a book," Aunt Harriet said, more than once. When autumn declined into winter, I did just that—wrote my experiences up in the form of a novel, with the sort of sentimental heroine my cousins seemed so fond of. My hero, Lord Belvoir, was a combination made from the best parts of various officers I had known, topped off with a dollop of imagination. My heroine was pure fiction. If I ever met such a watering pot as Aurelia Altmire, I would give her a good shaking. The public, I say with mixed feelings, liked her monstrously. In two subsequent publications Aurelia straggled first through Portugal and Spain, then returned to England, where she was promptly set upon by a band of brigadoons worse than Boney's soldiers. With no thanks to herself, she came through victorious, bringing much unexpected wealth to her creator, who remained an anonymous English lady.

With my pockets jingling, I set off to the Orient to find more adventures for Aurelia, and for myself, Marion Mathieson. But I went also with the purpose of serious study to broaden my background. The book of memoirs presently on sale bears my own name, and gives some idea of what I have learned of foreign sights and customs. Miss Mathieson is highly respected in that widening circle of people interested in the East. One day I plan to settle down amongst the ton in London, and you may be sure they will never learn I am the authoress of the shameful Aurelia books. How Tom Moore would stare to hear such a thing!

And now at last we may return to the "excellent timing." Aurelia, once again being abused in fiction, was about to be set upon by highwaymen who planned to steal papers proving she was the legal but unacknowledged daughter of the Duke of Norval. I like to keep the details of my stories accurate, and had been lamenting to Ronald that I had somehow missed out on being held up by a scamp. With divine timing, the Lord God had heard me and come to my assistance. This has happened often enough abroad that I feel I am specially blessed by Him. I shall never forget the night my party was ambushed by Bedouins in the desert. In that god-forsaken spot, where a white man is seldom seen, a very dashing German gentleman came galloping to our rescue. Lord Belvoir will soon have a dueling scar over his left cheekbone, thanks to Herr Grimmel. It will turn white when he is angry, and pink when he is pleased with Aurelia.

Naturally, I was not about to sit on my thumbs when we were being attacked by highwaymen. Ronald opened the door and we both clambered out. There were three of them; one remained mounted, and the others had dismounted to haul the coach driver and our outside passenger to the ground. Our coachman held his left shoulder with his right hand. I assumed the shot had hit him, but he didn't appear to be in terrible pain. The passenger was being ordered to turn out his pockets. To encourage obedience, all the highwaymen had their pistols drawn, cocked and aimed. Vision was blurred due to the pelting rain, but I could at least see that the scamps on foot were not large men, though they were wiry. They all wore masks and hats pulled low over their foreheads. The passenger looked fairly bored as he handed over his money purse without a word of disagreement. Lord Belvoir would not be so pusillanimous when his turn came. His scar would blanch and his eyes darken to slits.

Not satisfied with the purse, one of the bandits touched the muzzle of his pistol to the passenger's heart. "Open your jacket," he said, in a voice that menaced dire results if disobeyed. I discovered that our new passenger had two expressions. Bored and more bored. Wearing his more bored face, he pulled the coat back to display a sprigged waistcoat. "Now the waistcoat," our bandit ordered. The passenger began slowly removing his York tan gloves. The bandit pushed his hands aside and pulled from beneath the waistcoat a letter. A dark blot on it appeared to be a wax seal. The slit of mouth beneath the mask curved in a satisfied smile, and the letter was handed to the mounted scamp.

I began to think it was that letter and nothing else the highwaymen wanted. What could be in it? The highwaymen then turned their attention from the languid Adonis to Ronald and myself. "Hand over your blunt," one said.

"My reticule's in the coach," I replied. "I'll get it." I intended to dump most of my money before giving it to him, but apparently the scamps were aware of that stunt, for one of them followed me closely.

Once at the carriage door, they discovered Reverend Cooke and Mr. Wideman, cowering in a corner instead of coming to our aid. The highwayman hauled them out into the rain and entered the carriage himself. He was soon out carrying my leather lap case, Wideman's sample case, and the reverend's book. What he had missed, however, was my little patent reticule, which must have been overlooked at the back of the seat. All the stolen articles were dumped into a sort of leather pouch affair hung over the highwaymen's mounts. While one of them cleaned out the carriage, the other ordered Cooke and Wideman to stand and deliver. They handed over their money without a word.

The money was added to the leather pouch. One of them murmured something under his breath. It sounded like "Chev o" or possibly "Shove oh." He then went to the carriage team and set them free, hitting their rumps with the harness to make sure they ran off on us. The three scamps exchanged a complimentary smile, gave a Gallic shrug of their shoulders, and one of them decided to be gallant. He lifted my hand and kissed a very wet glove. "Mam'selle." He bowed, and hopped on his horse.

It wasn't a terribly exciting performance. I had expected better of the highwaymen—and the passengers. Other than that final kissing of my hand, I began to think I could write a better scene for Aurelia myself. There had been no brutality, no roughing up of the passengers—possibly because they had all acted as tame as rabbits. I remembered the groom's wound and turned to help him.

Before I took a single step, the new passenger strode up to me and stood glowering down from his six feet and a few inches. I measure five feet eight myself, and was not likely to be intimidated by a tame English cow-

9

ard after doing business with Emir Mohanna, the Bedouin chief, and the dreaded Turkish Pasha Suliman. The Turkish pashas had been known to remove the nose, one eye, and one ear of a previous visitor.

"May one enquire why you got out of the carriage, madame?" he sneered, in an accent I wouldn't use to the lowliest *saice*. "You made it impossible for us to defend ourselves, with a lady present."

"Is that your excuse for tugging your forelock and handing your money over to common thieves?" I replied tartly. The drooping eyelids lifted a fraction, revealing a flash of anger. "Five of you men against a mere three of them! I assure you the lady would have a better opinion of you had you defended yourselves—and her." The gentleman looked taken aback at my answer, but I elbowed him aside and took a look at the groom's arm.

"Am I dying?" he asked fearfully.

"If you'll get in the carriage, I'll tie a handkerchief around this scratch. Fortunately, you were only grazed. Ronald, you'd best go after the team, as it's clear no one else here has his wits about him."

Ronald provided a handkerchief before leaving, with the chastened passenger in tow. I took the groom into the carriage and did what I could in the dark to provide him a dressing. "Do you coach drivers not carry a gun?" I asked.

"The shot came out of the dark and winged me before I could draw. I wasn't looking for scamps on a night like this."

"Surely a moonless night is the likeliest time for attack?"

"Moonless, not bloody pouring rain!"

"How about the man sitting on the perch with you?"

"Kestrel was driving. The bucks like to take the reins."

I was familiar with this strange desire on the part of

sportsmen to play at being coach drivers. "Is that his name?" There was, in fact, a hawkish quality to the man's face—something in those hooded eyes—but he was no small hawk. More an eagle than a kestrel.

"It's a title," the groom replied. "Kestrel's a lord, one of the Corinthian set."

Oddly enough, Ronald had been urging me to ingratiate myself amongst the nobility. There was some discussion the other night about my receiving an order for meritorious public service. Were I a gentleman, Moore felt, I would certainly have been knighted. I would have been well pleased with a lesser token of recognition. Not anything so exclusive as the Most Noble Order of the Garter, but some sovereign recognition of my accomplishments. My being a female was all that prevented it, according to people who know more about such things than I. Only strong noble connections could induce Prinney to reward a lady. It seems the only honor a lady may receive is a pat on the head, unless the sovereign decides to go whole hog and create her a peeress in her own right. This is about as likely as the sky falling in. In any case, I had scotched any possibility of Kestrel's setting up a lobby to gain me a meritorious order.

"How far are we from civilization?" was my next concern.

"Chatham's ten miles ahead."

"There must be something closer than that."

"There's a stretch of hop farms hereabouts. You must have seen the oasthouses—them with the pointed roofs."

I had noticed this feature during the latter part of the afternoon. "We'll go to one of the farms if the gentlemen can't recover the team."

"They'll not catch Maggie and Belle. Them mares like their freedom too well. Pity it's raining so hard."

Mr. Wideman and Reverend Cooke joined us, and

the discussion turned on their loss. Mr. Wideman figured he had lost five guineas worth of toys, and the reverend lamented the loss of his book (i.e., pictures). In actual cash, he had lost only a couple of guineas.

"How much did you lose, ma'am?" Cooke asked me.

"I lost nothing," I announced, and retrieved my reticule from behind the groom, where it had gotten wedged in below the squabs.

"You're lucky you had on your gloves, or they'd have pulled off that dandy ruby ring," Wideman mentioned.

"I have twenty-five guineas in my reticule, too," I said, congratulating myself on its deliverance.

"It's strange they didn't demand our watches," Wideman said, massaging his generous chin. "I've lost two watches to the scamps."

"They didn't seem to notice my reticule was missing either, but it's my ruby ring, a present from Emir Beshyr, chief of the Druses, that I'm especially glad to have safe."

"Would it be amiss if I asked what a Christian lady was doing amidst such foreigners?" Wideman asked.

I mentioned a few of my milder exploits, and at length Ronald and Lord Kestrel returned, empty-handed. "I knew how it would be," the groom said, shaking his head. "They've bolted to Chatham on me."

"You might have told us, my good man, and saved us a highly uncomfortable slog through the mud," Kestrel suggested, still bored.

The rain hadn't let up. As the carriage was full, the new arrivals stood at the door, with their heads in out of the wet. We discussed for a moment what was best to be done. Ronald spoke of walking to the closest farm and trying to borrow a team. The groom thought the closest place likely to have horses was three miles ahead.

"It would take hours!" I pointed out. "The rest of

you may do as you please, but I intend to walk to the closest house and seek refuge.''

Without further ado, I had Ronald unfasten my small case from the top of the rig, put my pelisse over my head like a blanket to protect my bonnet, and was ready to go. The others grumbled themselves into agreement with my idea, and together the six of us lit out into the teaming rain, peering into the shadows for a sign of more attackers.

Chapter Two

There are many sorts of people in the world, and the sort with whom Ronald and I had fallen into company were the sort who hug their misery to their breasts in silence. In vain did I urge our companions to sing, and alleviate the discomfort of plodding through the dark, wet night.

"There is a season for all things, Miss Mathieson," Reverend Cooke said, in a damping way.

"And this is *not* the season for merry song," Lord Kestrel added, rather conclusively.

After an hour Mr. Wideman finally opened his lips. "I'm starved," he muttered.

"You can afford to lose a few pounds," I told him. The man could drop two stone and be the better for it.

"It's perishing cold," Reverend Cooke added half a mile later.

"I'm soaked through" was Kestrel's addition to the lament. "I fear Weston's jacket is beyond repair."

Even Ronald turned pessimist on me. "I haven't been this wet since we were shipwrecked off Rhodes," he said.

I said nothing, but as with our shipwreck, which endured eight hours, my own major concern was food. In a last effort to brighten the journey, I turned to the groom. "You must be our *saice*, our guide, sir. How much further do you figure we must go?"

"A long ways yet" was his uninformative reply.

The rain was so heavy that I felt it seeping through my pelisse to dampen my shoulders. The last thing I wanted was a feverish infection, with my lecture tour set. When I spotted a dark hulk ahead of us, I pointed it out. "What is that?"

"It looks like a hop-picker's hut," the groom replied.

As we drew nearer, it proved to be slightly more than a hut. It was a small cottage, not at all prepossessing, and with no outbuildings hinting at horses, but it had a roof over it, and we all turned as one toward it. I felt a moment's pity for the poor farmer's wife who would have to spread her meager hospitality over so many of us. Kestrel's concern for his jacket finally shook him out of his lethargy. He took the lead. He advanced and knocked so loudly, the door rattled. Then we waited. A moment later he knocked again, if kicking a door with a booted foot can be called knocking. Still there was no reply.

"Are they deaf!" he exclaimed, and took hold of the handle to rattle the door loose. He strode in and bellowed, 'Hello' a couple of times. There was no reply. "It's empty," he told us.

This seemed to be the case. We all straggled into the pitch black, and still there was no sign of life. "We need a light," he decided.

"Ronald, go out and see if you can detach one of the carriage lamps," I suggested.

The groom went with him, and they soon returned, each carrying a lamp, which by good fortune were of the old detachable sort. The room we stood in was a combination dining and sitting room. It had a dusty deal table and two lopsided chairs, a lumpy horsehair sofa with half the stuffing on the floor, a sideboard, and a grate with a half-empty basket of wood beside it. "Does anyone know how to light a fire?" I enquired.

The gentlemen exchanged startled looks at the suggestion that they should lift a finger for their own comfort. The faces soon turned toward the groom. "John Groom is wounded. Surely one of you knows how to start a fire!" I scolded. "Ronald?" He went to the grate and dumped the container of wood in.

"You need room for a draft, and a bit of kindling or paper to get her started," the coachman suggested. He directed Ronald to build the wood up in a certain order. I found some old newspapers which I formed into balls while the gentlemen looked on, and with a light from the lamps, we eventually got a small, smoky fire going. We received very little heat from it, however, as we all hung our coats on the chairs to dry in front of it. This left the horsehair sofa, holding three at the most, for our only seating.

The noble gentleman was the first to avail himself of a seat, with the vicar not a step behind him. Wideman took a look around and soon legged it to grab the other spot. I cast a disparaging glance at the three rude brutes and said to Ronald, "It is a great comfort to be surrounded by *gentlemen* at this time of difficulty. Reassuring to know their high opinion of ladies goes beyond failing to defend her during a holdup."

Kestrel stared at me from his cold gray eyes, still drooping in boredom, and shuffled to his feet. "Would you care for a seat, Miss Mathieson?" he asked wearily.

"Thank you, sir," I replied, and with a frosty look, sat down, shivering and rapidly becoming weak from starvation.

My companions seemed to have taken the notion that I was in charge of affairs, and asked what should be done. "We'll need more firewood before long. And as this rain shows no sign of letting up, someone ought to go and see if there are any bedrooms or blankets in this shack.''

The cottage was only one story high. It had one bedroom in the back, empty save for a roll of tattered, foul-smelling blankets on the floor. Ronald brought them for my inspection. "Goat blankets," I said, waving them away. I recognized the odor from Damascus. Kestrel's nostrils quivered in distaste, and he fanned the air beneath his nose with his curled beaver hat. Only John Groom, whose name was in fact Mostly, availed himself of the blankets.

"If we had some boiling water, I'd cleanse that wound properly for you, Mostly," I told him. The gentlemen looked around the room, everywhere but to the black pot sitting by the grate. "Would someone care to see if there's a pump in the kitchen?"

I directed this civil request to Kestrel, who gave a silent sneer, but he went forward stiffly and took up the pot. I feared he would not clean it first, and went after him, taking a lamp with me. The kitchen was a discouraging sight. There was a pump in the corner and an open hearth, but they were the extent of its facilities. "That pot should be scoured before you fill it," I told him.

"What would you suggest I use to scour it? My bare hands? There's no brush here." His languid tone was becoming testy.

"Is your handkerchief clean?"

He pulled out an immaculate handkerchief, wet it from the pump, and rubbed it around the inside of the pot before filling the latter. He then carried the pot and hung it over the fire, which by this time was petering out. "We need more wood for the grate," I said.

He looked at the empty wood basket. "There doesn't seem to be any more. Perhaps those chairs—"

"They don't belong to us. There must be a woodshed

attached to this cottage. Let us see if they left any wood behind.''

Kestrel leapt to attention, surprising me by the quick movement. ''Aye, aye, sir!'' he exclaimed, and saluted. Wideman emitted a chuckle from the sofa. I paid no heed to this puerile attempt at humor, but went back to the kitchen, Kestrel following me. We found a low door leading into a woodshed. Unfortunately, the roof leaked, so that the top wood was quite sodden.

''No doubt you have a plan for me to dry this soaking wood?'' he asked. ''I'm eager to hear it.''

His sarcasm was ignored as thoroughly as his poor attempt at humor. ''That won't be necessary. It will be drier below, if you would be so kind as to remove the top couple of layers.''

A muscular spasm around his mouth was the only sign of revolt. Kestrel pulled away the top layer to discover dry logs beneath. They were enormous pieces of tree trunk.

''We'll need a team of horses to get these into the living room.''

''They'll have to be chopped,'' I pointed out reasonably.

''Of course,'' he said, all fight gone. His elegant shoulders sagged to consider the chore in front of him. He inhaled slowly, looked around the shed, and found, to his dismay, a rusty axe leaning against the wall. He took it clumsily in his hands and began battering at the tree trunk. When he finally made contact with the stump, he imbedded the axe so firmly in it that he couldn't get it out. ''What now?'' he asked, with a gleam of satisfaction, thinking he had made the job impossible of completion.

''I suggest you remove the axe blade and try again.''

He straightened up, arms akimbo, puffing from his exertions. ''My name is Lord Kestrel, ma'am, not King Arthur.''

With one hand I gently pushed him aside and showed him how to hold the stump steady with one foot while applying pressure upward on the axe handle with both hands and jiggling to extricate the blade. This done, I passed the axe to him. "Excalibur awaits your pleasure, sir."

He took it without a word and raised the axe to repeat his error.

"Excuse me," I said, and took the axe from him. "I spent a month one winter in the Syrian desert, which to my surprise, had six inches of snow and was extremely cold. It was very pretty in summer, however, with mountains, hills, and green plains, dotted with flowers and herbs. By 'desert' the Syrians mean only a place without houses. In any case, I have seen the natives chop wood and learned how to do it." I placed a stump in the ground, leaned the smallest log I could find against it, and aimed not for the middle of the top log, but a point a few inches in from the outside. It split with a satisfying snap, and a piece of wood flew across the room. That it happened to hit Kestrel was an accident.

"You'd best stand back a little," I advised, and raised the axe again. When I had chopped the first trunk into burnable pieces, I handed Kestrel the axe. "Do you think you have the knack of it now? We shall need half a dozen more logs chopped up."

"An impressive performance, Miss Mathieson." He bowed, and took the axe. I collected up my pieces and went to build up the fire. From time to time Kestrel came and deposited an armful of chopped wood at my feet, like a magpie bringing chips of glitter to its mate. I did the civil thing and said, "Thank you" on each occasion. When the pile was higher than necessary, and when Kestrel was gasping from exhaustion, I said, "That will be enough for tonight. You'd best sit down

19

or you'll have a stroke. My, you're not as hardy as you appear. Have you been ill, Lord Kestrel?"

"I was feeling fine till tonight," he said through clenched teeth. Then he went to the door and looked out. The rain was still coming down in buckets. Despite this, he took his steaming coat from in front of the fire and put it on.

"You're not leaving!" I exclaimed.

"Sorry I can't remain to kill a wild boar or a bear for dinner, or perform whatever other chores you desire, but I am in rather a hurry. I have every confidence you will manage without me. Good night, Miss Mathieson. It has been . . . educational meeting you."

He clapped his curled beaver on the side of his head and left. I figured his fit of pique might get him the length of a city block. I underestimated his stubbornness. He wasn't back for half an hour, by which time he was soaked through and sneezing, and I had cleansed Mostly's wound and got more water on to boil. "I must have walked in a circle. I ended up here again," he said with a sheepish glance.

"It's difficult to navigate when the stars aren't out," I conceded, and took his coat to place by the fire with the others.

The subject of dinner was at the back of all our minds. It was Wideman who gave it voice. "I wonder if there's any food in the pantry," he said, casting a hopeful glance at myself.

"Why don't you have a look?" I suggested.

He was still looking five minutes later, by which time impatience won and I went to join him. Kestrel wandered out behind me. He wore an expression of doubtful curiosity.

"What we've got is a tin of coffee and half a tin of flour," Wideman announced. "Can you do anything with that, Miss Mathieson?"

"Pity it weren't a loaf and fishes," Kestrel said. "But

I have no doubt Miss Mathieson will contrive a meal from that inauspicious beginning.''

''We can have coffee at least.''

''With no milk and sugar?'' Wideman asked, offended.

''If you would care to run along to Chatham and do some shopping, sir, we can have milk and sugar with it. You might as well pick up some bacon and eggs while you're there.''

I took the tin of coffee and rattled through the cupboards, looking for cups and a coffeepot. I found an old enameled pan, put the coffee in it and poured the boiling water from the grate on top. That was our dinner, served in wretched old chipped cups without handles. It tasted very good, too. I was accustomed to taking my coffee straight in my travels. At least it was hot.

''I could go for a beefsteak right about now,'' Mr. Wideman said, licking his lips.

Kestrel nodded in sympathy. ''I had some hope Miss Mathieson could bake us up a few loaves from that tin of flour, as I'm sure is done in the deserts of Arabia.''

''Of more importance,'' the vicar announced, ''is how we are to spend the night. I suggest we give Miss Mathieson the bedchamber, and we gentlemen roll up here in these smelly blankets before the fire. That weather isn't fit for man nor beast.''

''Very kind of you, Reverend,'' I said, ''but you may take the freezing bedchamber. I'll sleep on the floor by the grate with the rest of them.''

''But you're a lady!''

''And you all, I trust, are gentlemen?'' My scathing glance included even Mostly, who sat on the floor like a dog, scratching his ear.

''We are none of us brave enough to molest Miss Mathieson,'' Kestrel announced, with an unnecessarily sly grin at my predicament. ''I suggest we give her the sofa, while we all roll up in our coats and sit out the storm. If anyone is able to sleep under such conditions, more power to him. I shall be awake, and will undertake to guard Miss Mathieson's honor—with axe, if necessary."

"Take note of that, gentlemen. I promise you, if once Lord Kestrel imbeds the blade in your head, it is there forever."

We were all too tired and hungry to argue. I lay down on the sofa with my damp pelisse over me, and soon the men gathered around the grate, trying to get comfortable. For an hour I lay awake, wondering why I couldn't sleep in the relative comfort of this cottage. I had slept under worse conditions, often on the ground, surrounded by Arabs who would as soon slit your throat as steal your gold. What I mean is that it wasn't the discomfort, and certainly not fear of being molested by any of these tame fellows, that kept me awake.

I kept thinking of the highwaymen, and the lackadaisical way they had robbed us. Surely professional bandits would have taken our watches and rings. They would have remembered my reticule. They wouldn't have kissed my hand, and called me mam'selle. That "mam'selle" hinted at French attackers. With an invasion from Napoleon imminent, the French were much in everyone's mind. This opened a new avenue of exploration. Why had they singled out Kestrel for a closer examination than the rest? They had looked very smug when they found that letter in his waistcoat. Was it no ordinary letter, but something to do with Boney? A strange place to carry a letter, next to the heart, as it were. Or was it merely a billet-doux? Strange to think of that dour, lazy-eyed man being in love. What would she look like? I pictured a wilting violet, some demure, prissy young lady—pretty, of course, in the conventional mold.

I was never called pretty. A Greek professor of art

once used the phrase "Hellenic beauty" to describe me. He said I had a classical face, by which I believe he meant a certain regularity of features, and perhaps a statuesque quality, due to my height. Men stare at me, but to be realistic, which I always endeavor to be, I think there is more surprise than admiration in their gaze. I saw plenty of that abroad.

I often thought of my travels while I lay in bed at night. Home again in England, I would remember the mountains of Lebanon, and Emir Beshyr's mountaintop palace, where we drank sherbets and he taught me to smoke his nargileh. And the old sheikh's palace at Maktara, where a stream of mountain water flowed through all the rooms, giving off a silver tinkle as it ran over the stone floors. And of the desert emir, Mohanna el Fadel, who called me *Meleki*—the Queen. It was my fair coloring and blue eyes that interested those easterners, that and the fact that a European lady traveled amongst them. I was the first one most of them had seen. How they came to stare! Thousands of them would meet me at the entrances to their towns. I had been treated royally by pashas and emirs, by princes and sheikhs, but in England, a lord did not treat me with even common respect. Kestrel had been mocking me since our arrival here. Perhaps that was what kept me awake. I glanced at the roll on the floor where Kestrel was lying, and noticed it move.

He sat up and looked around. Then he rose and began piling wood on the smouldering fire. The flames shining up on his face gave him a demonic air, like Lucifer. It played over his deep-set eyes and traced shadows on his lean cheeks. I was attracted by that air of danger the fire conferred on him. Kestrel pulled out his watch, went to the door, and frowned at the curtain of rain that still came down. I remembered the questions that had plagued me earlier, and decided this was the time to find some answers.

I got quietly up from the sofa, pulled my pelisse around me abba-style, and went softly forward. "You're still awake!" he exclaimed.

"Shhh! I don't want to wake the others. Come to the sofa a moment."

A leap of astonishment lit his pale eyes. The idiot thought I was planning to seduce him! "I have a few questions I'd like to ask," I said. Ignoring that brief misunderstanding seemed the best way to handle it.

Kestrel was less subtle. "That's a relief!" he murmured.

"Ah, you feared I was after more wood. There's plenty to last till morning." I sat demurely on one end of the sofa, Kestrel as far away from me as possible. "I find it peculiar the highwaymen left so many valuables behind, don't you?" I began.

"The weather might account for their haste."

"It's surprising they were out in such weather at all. Mostly found it unusual. But being out, why did they not collect our jewelry—and my reticule?"

"Are you complaining that they missed a few items?" he asked.

"Not complaining precisely, but it is odd. *You* are the only one they actually searched," I added pensively.

"I should think the cut of Wideman's jacket was enough to disqualify him. And a vicar wouldn't be carrying any money."

"Cut bait, Lord Kestrel. It was that letter hidden under your waistcoat they were after. The rest of it was a sham to make us think it was a regular highway holdup. What was in that letter?"

"It was a personal matter."

"Highwaymen don't steal billets-doux. You were coming from London toward Dover. The coast is expecting a visit from Boney any day now. Is it possible you were carrying a missive from Whitehall to the army stationed at the coast?''

"You have an active imagination, Miss Mathieson.''

"I didn't imagine that they called me mam'selle, and that they said '*chevaux.*' I didn't quite catch it at first, but immediately after he said it, the bandit cut the team loose. That's what he said—*chevaux.* In case you aren't aware of it, Lord Kestrel, *chevaux* is French for horses. Are you a . . . spy?'' My voice rose on the last word. What astonished me was not that spies abounded at this time and place, but that such an incompetent sort of gentleman as sat with me was of their number. First his curricle broke down, then he got held up, and instead of going after the enemy, he hung around this shack, chopping wood and drinking coffee. Really, it was incredible.

"What if I am?'' he asked.

"If you are, you'd best get after those Frenchies before they deliver your message to their superior. At least . . . I shouldn't think the ringleader was risking his life in a simple holdup. He'd have one of his minions do that.''

His chiseled nose pinched in annoyance. "Why do you think I left earlier?'' he demanded fiercely. He obviously didn't like to have his actions questioned.

"You found no trace of them?''

"You couldn't find St. Paul's in that downpour. As I said, I ended up walking in a circle. It seemed best to catch a few winks and be fresh to go after them in the morning.''

I nodded in agreement. "We must set out at the break of day,'' I said.

"We?'' Kestrel's eyebrows disappeared into his hairline, which was rather low on his forehead.

"There are three of them—unless they've met up with colleagues. You couldn't handle them alone when they held you up earlier. Obviously you need help.''

"I don't require the help of a lady."

"Try, if you can overlook your prejudice, and tell me truthfully, who do you think would be more help—the vicar and Wideman, or myself and Mr. Kidd?"

"The vicar and Wideman," he replied obstinately.

"Just what I have come to expect from you, Lord Kestrel, incompetence!"

I waited for his eyebrows to disappear again, and was surprised to see something like a smirk settle on his saturnine features. Of course, it is difficult for a kestrel to smirk, but the expression had that air of self-satisfied, superior amusement. "Wideman and the vicar were cowering like a couple of mice in the carriage when we were stopped by the scamps. Ronald may look ineffectual, but I assure he is an excellent shot, as am I. I always carry a pistol in my traveling case, and so does my secre—nephew. I also have a stiletto, and in a pinch can wield a rope to good effect."

"I am sure you could handle a mere trio of assassins. Naturally, I am relieved to learn Mr. Kidd can hold a gun. A pity you hadn't employed some of your arsenal during the holdup!"

"As I mentioned, I keep these items in my traveling case. In future travels, they will be closer to hand. I hadn't realized England had become so interesting during my absence."

A reluctant smile pulled his stiff face into a parody of civility. "Would it be ungentlemanly to suggest there is a cause-and-effect relationship?"

"On the contrary, I would take it as a compliment that my arrival generated any interest, but I fear that is bad logic on your part. A post hoc argument, if memory serves."

"It was not intended as a compliment," Kestrel said bluntly. "You, I take it, are the lady they call the Queen of the Orient? I have read something of your exploits in the London journals."

"That is mere propaganda put out by my publisher. Modesty forbids using the title myself, though it is true they greeted me as Meleki at Palmyra," I said dismissingly. "What we must do is make plans. A pity we haven't a map of the area."

"I have a map in my coat," Kestrel said, and reached in the pocket of his coat, which was around his shoulders for warmth.

We reignited one of the carriage lamps from the grate and, to avoid waking the others, took it into the one bedchamber. Lacking any furniture, we laid it flat on the floor and knelt down to examine it. On this occasion Kestrel did not put as much distance as possible between us. We knelt side by side. "We must be about here," I said, indicating our location with reference to Chatham. I noticed he had his own route marked out in red. As I had deduced, he was on his way to the army installations along the coast.

"Do you know what was in your letter of instructions?" I asked.

"I'm just a courier. If I knew that, I'd have continued on to deliver the instructions, and told the colonel they had been intercepted, so that he might make new plans."

"Should you not report your loss to Whitehall first?"

"That was my first thought. There isn't time. Those instructions were to have been delivered tomorrow."

"The highwaymen must have been delayed by this weather as well as we were. If we could hire some fast mounts and overtake them—"

"First I have to learn where they went."

"Use your head," I said impatiently. I noticed my brusque manner offended Kestrel, and spoke more gently to soothe his feathers. "French spies will be reporting to France. Naturally, they'll be heading for the coast."

"Somewhere between Dover and Bournemouth." He

puzzled over the map for a moment, then continued. "If you're really interested in helping, you and Mr. Kidd could take a message back to Whitehall for me, reporting the holdup, while I go after the spies."

"That news could go in the post. There's no urgency or danger in it. You have a hundred miles of coast to cover. Anything could happen to one man traveling alone. No, we must stick with you."

"It might be best if we all head east, but we'll split up. Your nephew and you go toward Bournemouth . . ."

The red line indicating Kestrel's route went straight as an arrow to Dover. "I hardly think Boney's men will go so far out of their way. The shortest route to France is Dover to Calais. To be on the safe side, however, we must cover the area from Dover to Dungeness. A little more than twenty miles, taking into account the coastal contours. We shall travel east together. If we don't overtake them before we reach, say, Ashford, then Ronald and I will go on to Dungeness, while you go to Dover and make your report to the colonel. I think that about settles it," I said, and got up from my knees, brushing the dust from my skirt and hands.

"You are certainly a lady who knows her own mind—and everyone else's," Kestrel replied. "Have you also decided how we are to obtain mounts? I have no money."

"I have plenty of that," I told him. The suspicion arose that he already knew my purse had escaped the robbers. Was that why he gave in to my persuasions? "I'm accustomed to traveling with a deal of cash. I adopted the habit during my travels. One never knows when she might have to hire a dozen guards or bribe a pasha or buy a camel. I can stand buff for the expenses. I am happy to do it, to help my country."

I could see Kestrel wasn't happy to be at my mercy, but he had only Hobson's choice in the matter. "Now that you've been robbed once, I don't have to point out the folly of carrying large amounts of money with you. You may not be so lucky another time," he said.

"I don't depend on luck. What I have learned from this incident is that I must buy a larger reticule, one that allows room for a small pistol. If I am ever asked to stand and deliver again, what I shall deliver is a bullet. It's shocking that a carriage holding four gentlemen plus a groom was defenseless against a couple of thugs."

"What shocks me, ma'am, is that they weren't defenseless against you."

"Experience, sir. I shall be better prepared another time, I promise you."

"The roads will be free of scamps in no time," Kestrel prophesied, in a satirical way that belittled my abilities.

He was not chastised for this innuendo, as my brain was active with a different notion. It occurred to me that this courier business Kestrel was involved in might prove interesting for myself, and Aurelia. Travel abroad was proving difficult during the war with Napoleon. Getting berth on a frigate depended as much on luck as connections. I might be sitting on my thumbs for months, and would enjoy the excitement.

"How did you come to win the job as courier, Lord Kestrel?" I asked.

"Win it?" he asked, eyes flashing. I feared I had unintentionally trod on the toes of his pride to suggest it had been gained in any other manner than by his abilities—such as they were. "I was coerced into it by Castlereagh. I needed his support for a bill I'm trying to get through Parliament, and to dilute his opposition—I can't use the phrase 'win his support,' as he hasn't lifted a finger to help me—I agreed to act as go-between for the government and the army."

This put a new complexion on the matter. Couriers,

it seemed, were actually in short supply! "I should be happy to do this sort of work myself."

"They don't employ ladies to do men's work."

"It's a pity men have requisitioned all the exciting jobs for themselves. Ladies would do nothing but sew and sip tea if they didn't infringe on men's prerogatives from time to time. Never having used a lady before is all the more reason to hire me. The Frenchies wouldn't be looking for any mischief from a woman."

He gave me a weary look. "The French, I believe, are more realistic in that respect. Since Marie Antoinette's causing a revolution, they have come to expect mischief from their ladies."

"This isn't the time or place for a lesson in history, though I expect you know where the fault for that revolution lies. I may be a woman, but I assure you, I could handle myself in any emergency."

"Spare me the details of your brawls with Arabs," he drawled, and drew out his watch. I did the same and saw it was half after five. "That rain seems to be letting up," he said.

The hammering on the roof had slackened to a patter, but it was still pitch black outside. "Let us hope it's stopped by daylight."

"Daylight? I plan to leave immediately—but if you would rather not—"

A glow of approval lit my face. "Well done, Kestrel! I didn't expect such alacrity from you." He took offense at this statement, which was intended as a compliment. "If the map we have been examining is accurate, we have a three-mile walk to the nearest village, and might arrive around daylight."

"If you want to give me the money, I'll go to Redden and hire mounts," he suggested.

"And waste another hour returning for Ronald and myself? No, it will be faster if we three go together. I'll waken Ronald."

Kestrel's grimace made me wonder whether he had any intention of returning for me and Ronald. I think he meant to dart off on his own. I quietly roused Ronald and told him what was afoot. He was accustomed to these little exploits and came without complaint. Indeed, he was as happy as myself to have something to do. Nor did he forget his position as my secretary. "What about your lecture tonight?" he reminded me.

"We should have taken care of the Frenchies in plenty of time to permit me to keep that appointment. I shan't postpone it yet, in any case. A pity I hadn't time for that practice run, but I have it down pretty well. They certainly seemed to like it in London. You must remind me to write to Tom Moore, Ronald. We were to set a time and place for me to go and look over his eastern poems."

Kestrel was standing impatiently while Ronald gathered up his things and my case. I delayed him only long enough to extinguish the lamp for safety's sake. This done, we silently opened the door and walked out into the night.

Chapter Three

The rain had slackened, but the countryside was so sodden, the trip had the sense of walking underwater, or through the sky. Fog drifted on the ground like clouds, wrapping us in mist to our necks, often giving no vision beyond our noses. We had to feel our way along the muddy road, looking out at any bend for a road sign. My slippers were destroyed, and the hem of my skirt clung to my ankles, impeding my steps.

"I wish I had my oriental trousers on," I mentioned to Ronald. "Skirts are impossible in such weather as this."

I felt rather than saw Kestrel's pinched face turn toward me in the fog. It was my wish to ingratiate the plague of a man to win his help in applying for a position as courier. To this end I explained a little further. "Adopting men's clothing during my trip was a necessity. We lost our trunks when we were shipwrecked off Rhodes. Naturally, European clothing was not available."

"Do they not have seamstresses in the East?"

"They do, but *La Belle Assemblée* is not available, so what the seamstresses sew is oriental clothing. I had either to dress like a Turkish lady, which meant wearing a veil and not speaking to any gentlemen, or dress like a man."

"Clearly it would have been impossible for you to curtail your conversation," he said. Without seeing his expression, it was impossible to know whether this was a joke, but I took it for an attempt at one and continued speaking.

"I found the men's full breeches very comfortable and convenient for riding."

Kestrel's voice came through the fog like a disembodied echo. "What else did you wear?"

"Several layers of shirts and waistcoats, all of it topped off with a short jacket—beautifully embroidered. They do magnificent embroidery in the East. There was a long sash—I needed someplace to stash my pistol and knife. And of course a turban for the head. One needs protection from the sun."

"I expect you and Lady Hester Stanhope got on famously," Kestrel mentioned.

"I never had the good fortune to meet her, though she was kind enough to send her Dr. Meryon to see me when I took a fever at Jerusalem. He brought me some lovely oranges and watermelons. I brought some seeds of the latter back with me. I think they might grow in an orangery. Delicious fruit."

"What was your impression of Jerusalem?" Kestrel asked. I think that despite his brusque manner, he was becoming somewhat interested in my journey.

"We visited all the holy places. The Holy Sepulchre was small and insignificant. Only four of us could get in at a time. We kissed the marble slab that covers the grave. I regret to say the place abounds with ignorant superstition. A footprint was pointed out to me as supposedly having been made by the Holy Virgin. It looked like a man's bootprint to me. In fact, when Ronald put his boot in it, it fit perfectly."

"Did you travel the route from Gethsemane to Calvary?"

"Indeed we did, and a hard trek it was, even without

the weight of a cross. I brought home what purports to be a sliver of the cross, but I fancy if all the slivers were put together, we would have a veritable forest. If you are interested in these matters, Lord Kestrel, I shall be delivering a lecture on my travels at Canterbury this evening at eight o'clock.''

"Where in Canterbury?"

"In the assembly room of the Fleur de Lis Hotel, in High Street. There ought to be signs posted announcing it. The proceeds will go to the church,'' I added, lest he take the idea I was trying to make personal profit from the lectures. "I have various artifacts in my trunk to be shown around—the sliver from the cross amongst them, along with a sample of the clothing I wore. Oh dear, I hope my trunk is safe on the coach! Surely Wideman and the vicar will attend to it when they awaken. I should have left them a note.''

"You actually overlooked a detail?" Kestrel joked. "I am mighty relieved to hear it. I was sure the redoubtable Miss Mathieson thought of everything.''

"With the assistance of her secretary,'' I added, to draw Ronald into the conversation.

"Why is it you require a secretary, Miss Mathieson?''

"For my writing,'' I answered vaguely, and quickly moved to a less prickly topic. "Your groom, I should think, will take care of your curricle and personal effects?''

"Of course.''

"That was a bang-up team of grays, Kestrel. How did you come to break down?" Ronald asked.

"I didn't break down. The curricle was new. I believe, and my groom agreed with me, that the pin was damaged on purpose by the French spies before I left London. It appeared to have been partially sawed through, to ensure breaking within a few miles. It made stealing my letter easy, away from the city, you know.

They must have been loitering a little behind us. Fortunately, the stagecoach came along before they arrived. Not that it made much difference in the long run."

"If you knew all that, what you should have done was give the letter to your groom," I said. "They would think you had it, and he might have delivered it without trouble."

"A pity I hadn't met you at the time to explain these matters to me," he answered stiffly.

Conversation petered out after that exchange. I refused to be baited into a riposte. I would win this arrogant devil's goodwill if I had to swallow a quart of spleen in the doing. As we progressed, the fog dissipated. After an hour or so, a weak ray of sunshine peeped through the cloudy heavens and gave us a view of the countryside. Kent, along with a few other counties, is called the Garden of England, and in the spring the title seemed appropriate. Fruit trees were in blossom, conferring some beauty on the cottages, which were a hodgepodge of flint and stone, timber and brick. Kent has only flint as a native building material, and as it is hard to work, the Normans often shipped stone across the channel. The result is quaint, picturesque, uniquely English.

Men were already at work in the hop fields, where the vines had crawled halfway up the strings supporting them. The plentiful light green of new bines hinted at a good season for the growers. Oasthouses were there in abundance. Some farmers had a few sheep grazing. I mentally turned each into a roast of lamb, for I was quite hollow from hunger. I thought Kestrel might mention stopping at one of the cottages for breakfast, but as the sun gave better vision and the road firmed under us, he only picked up the pace till we were nearly galloping toward Redden, the village we had chosen as our first stop.

At length we espied a low stone church in the distance, and knew the village was at hand. It was seven-thirty—the trip that should have taken less than an hour had taken two. I trusted Kestrel was not so superhuman that he meant to begin the search without first having breakfast, but I left it for Ronald to mention the subject.

"Thank God—there's an inn!" he exclaimed. "I'm hungry as a camel."

We all found new vigor to increase the pace. It was like a horse race to see us all bolting at breakneck speed toward the hanging sign that symbolized food. The place was called the Redden Maids, and the sign showed two ladies joined at the hips, though I believe this unusual set of twins were—was?—actually from Bidden-den, if memory serves. Ronald held the door and we entered into a modest but clean establishment. The air was filled with the aroma of coffee and gammon frying. How the mouth watered!

Kestrel let out another of his hello's, and a man appeared. "Good day, sirs." He smiled. "Mr. Monahan at your service. Can I offer you a table—the private parlor by chance?" he asked hopefully, as he caught a view of myself. I hadn't quite kept pace with the gentlemen as the hope of food drew near, but it was not for lack of trying.

"If you please," Kestrel said.

We were led into a small parlor, where a welcoming fire was just beginning to catch on. At closer range, Monahan noticed our disheveled condition, especially my own pelisse, and enquired if we had had a breakdown.

"We've been walking for hours," Kestrel told him. "We were held up by highwaymen last night."

Monahan shook his grizzled head. "I smelled trouble when that pair of ill-natured mares wandered into town this morning, after the coach not coming through last night. I had thought it might be the weather that held it up. We've never had any trouble with the scamps here-abouts. Held up, eh? Did you lose much?''

"Nothing of account, but the young lady has her trunk on the coach, and must recover her things.''

"I'll send word to the constable and have him go after the coach. Was the driver kilt?''

"No, wounded. He's safely housed a few miles down the road. You didn't have three shifty-eyed ne'er-do-wells turn up here last night or this morning? There were three of them.''

"They've not been seen in the village, or I'd have heard. Word gets around in a wee place like Redden. I'll keep an ear cocked for you, sir. Now, about break-fast . . .''

This important matter was taken care of, and while we awaited its arrival, we all hung our outer clothing before the fire. Our jackets were damp around the shoulders, too. "Let us dispense with formality and strip to our shirts," I suggested. "We don't want to take a chill when there's important work to be done.''

As Kestrel was kind enough to assist me with the removal of my traveling jacket, I returned the honor and helped him pull off his. His broad back stretched out above me. The shoulders, I noted with approval, were not eked out with wadding. When he turned around, his shirt was seen to be pulled taut across a well-muscled chest. The weathered column of his neck rose proudly against the white shirt. That latent streak of Aurelia in me felt a fleeting wish to spread her hands over his chest, to test its fibre. I looked up consciously and caught Kestrel examining my shirtfront with the same curiosity. Our eyes caught and held a moment. There was a tension in the air—a moment of acute embarrassment.

I turned away and busied myself arranging our jackets for the minimum of wrinkles, but I was minutely aware of his gray eyes following my movements. Soon we had a steaming plate of gammon and eggs, toast, and coffee before us, which we dispatched in short order. Conversation was nonexistent till our plates were empty. With only the coffee remaining, we resumed speech.

"I must try to find a new pair of slippers before we leave," I said. "Mine are like mashed paper. While you gentlemen finish your coffee, I'll dart over to the cobbler and see if I can beg or borrow something. I don't want to detain you."

I was able to beg a pair—red, alas!—of slippers made for a Miss Stone two years before. The lady had been dissatisfied with them, and there they sat, gathering dust till I rescued them. It was when I opened my reticule to pay that I discovered the stunt played on me. My money purse was missing! Either Mostly, the vicar, or Mr. Wideman had relieved me of my money. It must have happened while I was in the bedroom with Kestrel, for I hadn't slept a wink that night. Naturally I was furious with the thief, but of more importance, I had to part with a pretty little gold chain given me by the desert emir, Mohanna el Fadel. It was set with tiny emeralds and rubies, worth much more than the slippers, but I arranged to recover it for cash later. The theft also left us with the problem of settling up at the inn. I suspect that despite the inconvenience, Kestrel was not entirely sorry to find me bested by a mere merchant.

"I believe the thief was Wideman," I said angrily. "Mostly seemed a good fellow, and one can hardly accuse a vicar, even if he does carry pictures of partially draped women in his prayer book."

"Does he, by God!" Kestrel exclaimed, and laughed. "And he hadn't even the courtesy to share them with us. Well, Miss Mathieson, you have conned me properly. Here I let you come along so I could batten myself on your purse, and the purse is empty. That will teach me to cadge from ladies."

He spoke in jest, but I suspected there was an element of truth in his words, and of regret. Fortunately, Monahan was a generous man. He agreed to hold Kestrel's emerald ring till we could return. He was kind enough to advance several guineas in cash as well, to permit us to finish our journey. I was afraid Kestrel might try to hint us away now that he held the money, but he didn't mention it. During my absence the gentlemen had had their jackets pressed, their faces shaved, and their boots polished. They looked much more respectable than myself.

"Why don't you go to the stable and hire us a carriage while I freshen my toilette?" I suggested.

"A carriage?" he asked, surprised. "We can't hope to overtake mounted men in a carriage. I planned to hire mounts. But you're quite right. I cannot expect a lady to ride all day. I'll hire a carriage for you to continue to Canterbury, Miss Mathieson, while Mr. Kidd and I—"

"I'll ride," I said firmly.

"It will be very uncomfortable for you. We'll have to set a hot pace, probably for hours. And you're not outfitted for it either, in your gown and that pretty bonnet."

"I am wearing a comfortable traveling suit, not a gown. It will do for a riding habit. I'll leave my small case behind."

An obstinate glitter entered his steely eyes. "I must give you warning, I mean to hire the fastest horseflesh in the stable. Are you a good rider? Your experience on elephants will do you no good here."

"Camels are the beast of burden in the desert, Lord Kestrel. I ride a horse quite as well as I ride a camel, as Mr. Kidd will tell you."

"An excellent horsewoman," Ronald said at once.

"Very well." The curled beaver was clamped on his head, and he stalked out, leaving Ronald behind. During his absence, I tore the feathers from my bonnet to make it more suitable for riding, and turned down the brim to prevent its blowing off.

He was soon back with three frisky beasts, any one of which I was eager to get astride, though I assumed the smaller mare was intended for me.

"Silver is yours," Kestrel said with a challenging look, as he handed me the reins of the second fiercest animal. He kept the sturdy bay for himself. "They warned me she's raring for exercise," he cautioned.

My mare was a sleek animal, deep-chested, long-legged, silvery gray in color. "Thank you, Lord Kestrel. I wouldn't want to set out on a day's ride on a winded hack. This one reminds me of Zenobia, the mare Ibrahim Pasha loaned me at Damascus," I mentioned to Ronald.

"I hope you don't treat her the same way," Ronald laughed.

Kestrel looked interested to hear what accident had befallen me, but I silenced Ronald with a glare and mounted Silver without aid of either the mounting block or the gentlemen. It was a little awkward with my reticule over my wrist, but by no means impossible. And by the way, all that happened to Zenobia is that she slipped on a mountain road and sprained her ankle. It had nothing to do with the rider, but was solely the fault of the wretched road, all littered with stones and rocks, and very steep, too.

I was no sooner on Silver's back than she reared up on her hind legs and decided to unseat me. A restive whinny told me she was going to be trouble. There's no being polite with some animals, and I include human animals in that. I took my wrath with Kestrel out on Silver. Lacking a riding crop, I gave her a taste of the reins across her neck and jobbed at the bit. She settled down nicely and proved to be a sweet goer.

We figured our highwaymen had made for Chatham,

the closest city and the likeliest place for them to have stopped, if indeed they did stop before reaching the coast. With good mounts under us, we were at Chatham in no time. It was a bustling city, for Chatham has been one of the main naval and military stations since the days of Henry VIII. We weren't interested in such matters, nor in the pretty Medway River, but headed straight for the High Street. We enquired first at the Sun and Mitre for three travelers arriving late the night before. When they had no word on our thieves, we wasted considerable time at the smaller inns, but there was nothing to be heard of them.

"They didn't stop here at all," Kestrel decided. "They must have gone to Rochester or Gillingham. The three Medway boroughs are practically one town. I'm damned sure they didn't pelt all night through that downpour. It will take forever to find them."

"Let us continue toward Dover," I suggested.

Kestrel glowered and announced, "I'm in charge of this expedition." I just shook my head and waited for him to back down, for really, there was nothing else to be done. "*I* say we continue to Dover," he added, laughing to relieve his embarrassment.

We walked hastily along the High Street. A few of the merchants had stalls set up outside their door to lure passersby not wanting to go in out of the sun on such a fine day. My eye fell on a rack holding glass beads. I could swear I had seen those beads before. "Those are Wideman's trinkets!" I exclaimed. "Where did you get them?" I demanded of the clerk.

"These beads? Why, I bought them of a traveling salesman a month ago," he said. I took another look and could swear they were Wideman's stuff. They had the chip of red glass in the clasp. He had mentioned they were a new line, so how had the merchant had them a month? The man had a sly look in his eye. I didn't believe a word he said, but short of having him hauled off to a judge, there was no way of proving he was a liar, and time didn't allow me to call a judge.

"Just tell us when you bought them, and whether it was from three men," I said.

"I bought them a month ago," the clerk insisted.

"This is a waste of time," Kestrel decided. I remained a moment longer arguing with the clerk, trying first by threats, then cajolery, to get him to admit the truth. He stood fast in his story. When I looked up, Ronald had wandered along to another stall, but Kestrel was waiting for me, not patiently. He finally took me by the elbow and pulled me along.

"If you're convinced they're Wideman's trinkets, we know all we have to know. The Frenchies were here. We're on the right track. Now, where the deuce has Ronald wandered off to?"

He was half a block farther along with his nose in a book, his nose's preferred location. As it was my own book, *A Gentlewoman's Memoirs of the Orient*, he was holding, I didn't rush him, but waited to see if Lord Kestrel might be interested to pick up a copy.

"They have your book on prominent display, Marion," Ronald mentioned.

"Why, so they have! How nice. I wonder how it is moving."

Kestrel picked up one and leafed through it with a fairly disinterested face. "Is this any good?" he asked the clerk.

"I wouldn't know. I haven't read it. This one is a good mover," he replied. To my astonishment, he handed Kestrel a copy of Aurelia's adventures in Portugal. The infuriating man allowed his eyes to roam over those pages for much longer than he had given my memoirs.

"Good God, don't tell me you read such trash as this!" I was betrayed into saying.

He didn't remove his nose from the book, but reached

into his pocket to buy it. In my anger, I moved along to the far side of the rack, where used books were on sale. There, right on top, was Reverend Cooke's copy of the *Devotions and Sermons* of Dr. Donne. The pictures were still concealed inside. I quietly took it to Kestrel and showed him the name inscribed on the flyleaf. It was a gift to Cooke from the dean of Canterbury. "The vicar would be happy to have this back," I mentioned.

"He'll be glad to be rid of it," Kestrel thought. He took the book and shuffled the naughty pictures of the partially undraped ladies into his hand, thence into his jacket pocket. "I wouldn't want anyone to buy the book with Cooke's name in it and find these pictures," he explained.

"Make sure you don't put your name on the book they eventually end up in, in case you lose it like Cooke."

He turned his back to the stall and pulled the pictures out for examination. "They won't end up in a book. I'll have them framed for my study," he said, with a smile in his voice. That touch of lechery in him surprised me.

To mitigate the shame of the picture stealing, he bought a copy of my memoirs. With the books and the pictures strapped to his saddle, we were ready to go. We determined that one of the Frenchies had sold the stolen goods not two hours before. We figured out that the highwaymen had decided to make a small profit on the bits of loot stolen.

"We really ought to take a look around for your lap case, Marion," Ronald suggested.

I silenced him with a glance. I certainly didn't want Kestrel looking it over, with the latest Aurelia manuscript enclosed to embarrass me. "We can't waste a moment," I said hastily, and we were off to the coast. Of course, I would have to return and look for Aurelia later. I had three chapters done, and didn't want to lose them. I hoped no one would buy my lap case within twenty-four hours, but if they did, I could always discover the purchaser and send Ronald after her for the manuscript.

Kestrel set a hot pace along the road toward Ashford, where we were to separate, he going to Dover, Ronald and myself toward Dungeness. Orchards in bloom and pretty gardens whizzed past in a blur of white and pink. My years in various saddles, from camel to donkey to horse, stood me in good stead. If Kestrel hoped to see me tag behind, he was disappointed. I enjoyed every moment of it. When he paused to enquire whether I would like to stop for lunch, I assured him I could ride on for hours yet. We stopped at various villages to ask about our three highwaymen, and learned that we were gaining on them.

They had passed two hours ago, then one and a half, and finally one hour before us. This good news kept our spirits high. Kestrel could be an amusing companion when all was going his way. He came very near letting a compliment slip out as the morning advanced. "I take it you do a fair bit of riding?" he mentioned. (This was the near compliment. Look no further.)

"I have only three requirements in life. Food, a clean bath, and a good horse."

"You would hardly have had to go to the Orient for those basic needs."

"Naturally I was referring to physical requirements. The spirit makes its demands felt as well. Born a gentleman, you wouldn't be aware of the ludicrous restrictions placed on ladies."

"Most ladies find their entertainment in social doings—finding a mate first, and eventually marrying him and raising a family. Those more conventional pastimes didn't find favor with you?"

The use of the past tense with relation to marriage

surprised me. I never consciously ruled it out as a possibility. Rather than show my pique, however, I turned it back on himself. "Nor with you either, apparently, as you have chosen to remain a bachelor past the age when most men have settled down. Marriage is a contract devised by men, Lord Kestrel. In my view, they have kept the perquisites to themselves, and deposited the burden on the women."

"The financial burden is usually assumed by the gentleman."

"Yes, I have found a few gentlemen eager to assume the burden of spending my money under the guise of marriage."

A reluctant laugh rumbled in his throat. "You did the right thing to go to Arabia. You have the mentality of a peddler in a bazaar. I doubt if any gentleman will get the best of you in anything."

"Thus far, it hasn't prevented their trying." I am not actually so misogamistic as this speech indicates. I said it only to alert Kestrel that other gentlemen didn't consider me over the hill so far as marriage goes.

"I wouldn't want you to take the idea I'm angling after your fortune, Miss Mathieson," he said, and returned to business. "We're making good time. We can afford to stop for a quick bit of luncheon at the next village if you like."

"I can continue for another hour or so."

"Ronald is looking peaked," he decided. Since I wasn't hungry and he refused to admit he was himself, the chore fell to Ronald.

"We're only an hour behind our quarry. Would it not be better to push on till we overtake them?" I suggested.

Kestrel batted the idea away. "We're gaining steadily. They'll stop, and we should bait our horses, too. They'll be arrested before the sun sets."

The hindquarters do become fatigued, even on a

smooth-going mount. Without further argument, we agreed to pause for refreshment at the next likely spot. This proved to be a roadside tavern situated halfway between Chatham and Ashford. I lifted the menu and said, rather impatiently, "After such a hearty breakfast, we need no more than some cold cuts and bread here. We don't want to dally long. Will it be cold mutton for us all?"

Kestrel glanced at the bill of fare and was struck with a desire for roast lamb. He took considerable pains over his accompaniments. Was the asparagus fresh? How did cook do the potatoes? And what about a side dish of ragout to accompany the lamb? My menu rustled impatiently while I told Ronald he wanted only the cold cuts. Between the two of us, Ronald and myself, we glared Kestrel into leaving half his lamb on his plate—and it looked very tasty, too.

At last we were back on the road. The next time we got a whiff of our Frenchies, they had got an hour ahead of us again. "It's a pity we stopped!" I said, with an accusing look at Kestrel. We picked up the pace after that, but our quarry had got fresh mounts, and from then on, we didn't gain an inch on them till we stopped and got fresh mounts, too. Mine, I regret to relate, was a jaded, swaybacked old nag who shifted like a camel when she cantered. As we advanced toward Ashford, we lost the scent entirely. Our men hadn't been seen at the last two villages we passed through.

"There's obviously a shortcut we don't know about," Ronald thought. "We'll plough on to Ashford."

"If we don't stop to eat again," I said, with a commanding look to our leader, "We should overtake them there." Kestrel was sufficiently quelled that he didn't argue.

Chapter Four

We arrived at Ashford rather late in the afternoon. The town was a lively hunting center with some quaint old houses and a church boasting a fine perpendicular tower. The ride was not that far, but with all the stops to enquire for the Frenchies, we were considerably delayed. The difficulty now was to discover which route the Frenchies had taken—east to Dover, or south to reach the coast closer to Dungeness. This was the crucial moment, for if they took a side road to report to their masters here, we would never find them in time to recover the letter. I outlined my thinking to Kestrel as we entered the town.

"We'll make enquiries at the Saracen's Head and the Royal Oak. I'll take the former, you the latter," he decided.

"Would it not be wiser to ride through to the far end of town, and see if anyone saw them passing?" I countered. "They would not be likely to tell the innkeeper their route."

Ronald was glancing at his watch and finally spoke. "What about our lecture tonight, Marion? You should notify them it is to be postponed."

"Good gracious, it's not till eight o'clock, and Canterbury is only ten miles away. I'll be there. We'll have these fellows handed over to the authorities in plenty of time.''

"But you'll have to have a bath and change clothes. I think it would be wiser to postpone it. You won't have your box of souvenirs to show, or your Turkish costume—"

'Devil take it! It's not a sliver of an olive tree and a set of silk trousers they come to see. It's me! I'll be there. Oates would dislike for me to postpone the lecture when it's been advertised. Of more importance is catching the Frenchies. What do you say, Kestrel?''

"I'll just nip into the Saracen's Head and see if they've been there.''

As he was wasting time in this fruitless endeavor, Ronald and I went to the Royal Oak. "It seems to me Kestrel is dragging his heels,'' I scolded. "I begin to wonder if he isn't afraid to confront the Frenchies. He was only carrying that letter under duress, you know.''

It was only pique speaking. To my considerable astonishment, Ronald took up the theme and added some embroidery. "We could have caught them hours ago if he hadn't insisted on stopping for lunch.''

"Pest of a man! It's a shame to think the nation's safety is in such hands as his. After this is over, Ronald, I mean to apply to Castlereagh and offer our services as couriers—if you are agreeable, that is.''

I knew by the glow in Ronald's eye that he was in total agreement with me. "My papa knows a man who is acquainted with Melville, first lord of the Admiralty. He will put in a good word for us.''

"If we have success today, it will stand us in good stead.'' Success in catching the French spies became more important than ever.

The result at the Royal Oak was a blank stare. Dozens of men had been in and out all afternoon. The barkeeper couldn't remember three strangers having entered together, and if they had, they hadn't informed him they were carrying purloined letters to deliver to the French. We went to meet Kestrel outside the Saracen's Head. The aroma of ale lingered about him when he finally came out.

"No luck, I suppose?" I asked.

"On the contrary. Our quarry was there, and enquired for the fastest road to Dover," he replied, with great satisfaction.

I was more annoyed than happy that this dilatory spy should have met with success. "Fine, then we all hasten along to Dover."

"I think not. It will be better for your two to take the other road, in case it was a subterfuge. The road forks at the east end of town. We'll go together that far."

"You'll never be able to handle the three of them alone," I pointed out. Why that innocent remark should get Kestrel on his high horse was a mystery. "You don't even have a pistol," I added, to assuage his pride.

"That's a good point. I'll purchase one before I leave. The pawn shop is my best bet, since the money is running short."

"Did you leave London to deliver that important document without any protection?" Ronald asked. We exchanged a look, no longer of surprise at this poor excuse for a spy, but of dismay.

"I had a pistol in my curricle. I forgot to bring it along when I transferred to the coach," he admitted.

"You'd best buy two," Ronald said.

"That won't be necessary."

"If the Frenchies' asking for the Dover road was a subterfuge, as you suggested," I reminded him, "it is Ronald and myself who will have to deal with them."

Kestrel reluctantly acknowledged this, but when he came out of the shop, he carried only one pistol. "I didn't have enough money for two," he announced calmly.

"You got ten guineas for your emerald ring! You can't have spent that much!"

"There will be other expenses before we're through. I'm sure the Frenchies have headed straight to Dover. If you think you are on their scent, you should go to the constable here and seek assistance. It would be improper for a lady to mix with spies in any case."

It was too much to be borne. "Improper! You wouldn't be this close to them if a lady had not bullocked you into action, sir, and so I take leave to tell you. You'd still be on your haunches in some inn, eating mutton and leering at those dirty pictures you stole from the vicar and filling yourself with ale. This lady has dealt with rougher and more numerous enemies than a trio of tame Frenchies. I was betrayed by Prince Nasar and abandoned alone except for Ronald in the Bedouin desert, surrounded by Arabs who would as soon shoot us as spit. I brought them to heel, and I assure you I am not about to flinch from three damned Frenchies!"

Kestrel's nostrils quivered into slits. "It seems you hardly need a pistol, Miss Mathieson. You could quell them with no weapon save your sharp tongue."

"It's well my tongue is sharp, for if you shoot that pistol as incompetently as you do everything else, it will be yourself you maim. Come along, Ronald. We shall lay your watch on the wood and get ourselves a brace of pistols."

Ronald chose that moment to express his obstinacy. "Why not *your* watch?"

"Because I have already had to hawk my necklace. It's your turn."

While Kestrel stood trying to think of some clever set-down, Ronald and I went into the shop and, with our experience in Arabic haggling, managed to obtain the one remaining pistol in the shop, and the necessary ammunition, in exchange for Ronald's watch. "I wonder why Kestrel didn't take this one," Ronald said, hefting it. "It's well balanced—it looks brand-new."

"What would he know? His was probably a penny cheaper. He wants his money to buy ale."

Kestrel was still standing in the street when we came out. He looked at the pistol as though he would speak. I wasn't in a mood for more of his foolishness.

"Are you still here? What are you waiting for?" I scolded. "The Frenchies will have delivered their letter and sent it off to Boney. I begin to think that is precisely what you want."

As you have no doubt concluded already, I had given up any thought of using Kestrel as my entrée to Castlereagh. I was beginning to think Kestrel's help would do more harm than good.

His face turned scarlet with anger—or shame. He looked ready to explode, but when he spoke, he attempted a conciliatory tone. "I merely wished to settle how we should all meet up again after this business is settled."

"If we never meet again, it will be too soon for me. Good luck, Lord Kestrel. You'll need it."

On that brave speech I drew Ronald away and left Kestrel standing in the street with several hedge birds gaping at his disgrace.

"We shall send a note off to Canterbury after all, Ronald. I am too upset to give a proper speech this evening. Do you have any money?"

"The few shillings that were loose in my pocket when we were robbed. It should be enough."

We sent the message before leaving Ashford. This gave Kestrel a head start on us. By the time we reached the edge of town, there was no sight of him, which is just as well. My temper hadn't diminished since we parted ways.

"The man is a fool," I told Ronald. "He knew as long ago as yesterday when his curricle broke down that he was being followed. He should have left the letter for his groom to deliver. The spies wouldn't have bothered him. But no, what did he do? He climbed aboard our coach—without his pistol—and had us all robbed. And even then he calmly went to bed, instead of going after the men. Really, one trembles to think such dilatory men are our defense against Napoleon.

"As he knew he was being followed, you'd think he would have made some plans to defend himself—at least he could have hidden the letter a little better."

"He was too busy playing at coachman. Imagine, playing childish games at such a time. You know, I begin to think what we ought to do is follow him. The Frenchies will make minced meat of the man. It seems to me Dover is their likeliest destination. What do you think?"

"I found it suspicious they told the tapster where they were going. Of course, they couldn't know we were following them."

"It's the last thing they'd suspect, if they're familiar with Kestrel. Apparently they are. They cut his axle before he ever left London. There's a farmer checking his hay. Let's ask him if he happened to see three mounted men pass this way."

We dismounted and went to the fence to hail the farmer. Ronald has a way with provincials, and I let him handle the chore. "Good day, sir. That's a fine crop you have there."

" 'Twill be, after a bout of sun. The rain flattened her last night. Can I help you, sir?"

Ronald outlined our quarry. The farmer lifted his hat and scratched his head a moment. "I did see three bucks heading out Dover way a bit ago. The reason I noticed them in particular, they took the shortcut through my cornfield, the scoundrels. It cuts three mile off the main road, and meets up with it farther along. I hope old Ed Munster caught them and filled them with buckshot. They'd have to cross his barley as well. They leapt the fence and did considerable damage. I figured they must be local lads or they'd not know the shortcut, yet I didn't recognize 'em.''

"Were they dark-haired men, rather short?" I asked.

"They was on horseback. I couldn't judge their size, but they didn't look like big men. They was singing some song I didn't recognize—disguised, very likely. Maybe 'twas Gaelic. They speak queer in Wales, I've heard said.''

I thought more likely it was French. Spies working the area would know all the shortcuts, if they had their wits about them. I briefly outlined the situation to the farmer, and he gave us permission to leap his fence and destroy his cornfield. As I put my nag over the fence, my heart soared with her. We'd be ahead of Kestrel! Wouldn't he look nohow when he came upon us, with the Frenchies already captured! A farmer mending his fence, presumably Munster, let out a bellow as we plunged into his barley. We couldn't afford to stop. I hoped the other farmer would explain our trespassing.

When we met up with the road again, Ronald had lost his sense of direction. He wanted to turn west, but fortunately I was able to steer him toward the proper course. We rode hell for leather, keeping our eyes trained ahead for any sign of the three men. Riding sidesaddle felt wretchedly uncomfortable and inconvenient after riding astride in the desert. My full breeches there made that mode feasible. Riding astride was the least of my unconventional exploits, but one I didn't mention in my lecture. My publisher thought it might be considered unladylike! Really, the mind boggles to consider the inanity of convention.

We swept past dung carts and gigs, one handsome carriage with a lozenge on the door, and several mounted riders. The dust was negligible after the rain, so that was one annoyance avoided. It was just a few miles west of Dover that we spotted a lone horseman ahead of us. He was crouched forward, riding *ventre à terre*. We set our pace to overtake him, but the harder we rode, the harder it was to catch him. The man rode like a demon, and on an enviable black mount. I knew in my bones only an Arab stallion could set such a pace. "I wager he's one of the Frenchies," I gasped to Ronald, for the strain of a day in the saddle was beginning to tell. "Much chance that dolt of a Kestrel would have of outrunning him. Do you think we should follow him, or stop him and search him?"

"We'll never catch him," Ronald called back.

As he spoke, the man looked over his shoulder. I believe he knew we were chasing him, for he whipped his nag forward to a hotter pace. "We'll stop him. I'm certain he has the letter. Is the pistol loaded, Ronald?" He nodded. "Give it to me. I'm the better shot." Without breaking stride, he passed me the weapon. Ronald is a fair shot; he could have hit his target, but I wanted only to wound the man, not kill him, and that required better than fair.

We urged our steads forward ever faster, yet the man pulled farther ahead of us. We owed our eventual success to a jackrabbit. The helpful creature darted across the man's path, causing his mount to shy. By the time he got it calmed down, we were not three paces behind him. "Halt or I'll shoot!" I shouted.

The man's head turned slowly, and I found myself aiming a loaded and cocked pistol between Lord Kestrel's cold gray eyes. It was impossible, but there he was, astride the finest piece of horseflesh I had ever seen, and I've seen some handsome animals. His eyes seemed to shoot fire. Angry lines etched twin valleys from his nose to his thin lips. In my astonishment I heard myself say, "Where did you get that mount? That's not what you were riding."

"Don't point the pistol at him, Marion," Ronald said nervously. "It might go off."

My finger quivered with the urge to fire it. Kestrel's hateful smirk did nothing to alleviate the feeling. "Let her do her worst," he taunted.

I wasn't quite angry enough to kill him, but I meant to show him a lesson. I lifted the muzzle high enough to lift his hat from his head, and took aim. Kestrel must have known what I was doing, but he sat solid as a mountain, not even flinching. That only served to increase my wrath. I squeezed the trigger; nothing happened. It didn't move a millimeter. I squeezed again, harder, and still the trigger remained as unmoving as Kestrel.

"Next time you buy a gun, check to see the trigger hasn't been welded to prevent firing. That one's been fixed up as a room ornament. Why do you think I passed it up?"

I suffered a momentary lapse of sense and threw it at his head. He moved then, ducking to avoid being hit. "A display of childish temper from one of your years, Miss Mathieson?" He looked up to the sky. "I was sure it would be falling down on our heads from astonishment."

Ronald broke the tension by laughing. "The sky's seen her wrath before, Kestrel," he called.

After a moment's raillery at my expense, Kestrel's appetite for embarrassing me was assuaged and he returned to more important matters. "I thought you two were safely on the road south."

"We learned the Frenchies have definitely come this way, and we have come to help you," I told him, adding a little detail about the farmer.

Kestrel's words were only a growl in his throat, but had they been audible, there isn't a doubt in the world they would have been extremely profane. Rather than praising our efforts, he was as angry as a hornet that we were here. But as we were, we resumed the chase together.

"Where did you get that fine mount?" I repeated. "I can't believe such a treasure is hired out by an inn."

"I keep her at a little coaching house on the edge of town. I pass this way often, going between London and home."

"Then your home must be nearby. Where is it, exactly?"

"Not far from Margate," he answered curtly.

His mood didn't encourage any questions on this interesting subject. I was curious to hear more about the style in which he lived. "What's his name—the stallion's, I mean?"

"I call him Pegasus."

"The winged steed—well named! I shouldn't mind purchasing one of his brothers."

"Ladies can't handle a stallion. A mare or a gelding, perhaps."

"I have ridden camels in my time, sir, and not only tame hejyns either. I could handle Pegasus with one hand tied behind my back."

This proud boast was deemed beneath argument. Kestrel just gave me a disparaging look. I decided then and there that if I could not put Pegasus through his paces, I would put Lord Kestrel through his. By "could not" I mean had not the opportunity, not that I felt inadequate to the task. We continued on in silence for another mile. "We ought to be getting close by now. Do you think they've stopped? One of these farms outside Dover could be their headquarters," I mentioned.

Kestrel seemed impatient with us. "I suggest you and Mr. Kidd go into Dover—or on to Canterbury for your lecture. If you hurry, you can still make it. I'll handle it from here."

"I've already postponed the lecture. We will help you, and don't bother trying to get rid of us."

Kestrel reined up and turned to face Ronald and myself full on. "It's time to put an end to this charade. I know where the Frenchies are. I'll take care of it."

'How?" I answered hotly. "How do you suddenly know where they are when you haven't had a notion all day? And how will you handle them, all alone? I think you overestimate your abilities, sir. You hadn't the wits to take your pistol with you yesterday afternoon when you already knew they were after you, but amused yourself playing coachman instead."

Kestrel took a deep breath and finally decided to humor us with an explanation. "As I see you and Mr. Kidd have been discussing my ineffectualness as a courier, I might as well explain the situation. And as to ineffectualness, the only reason you're here, Miss Mathieson, is because I *thought* you had some money that would come in useful. Despite your self-endowed reputation for excellence in everything, you managed to lose it. I wanted to be overtaken and robbed yesterday. I knew when I examined my curricle before leaving London that I would be followed. Several messages of the sort I was carrying have gone astray recently."

"I'm not surprised," I threw in. "All the more reason to be prepared."

"None of mine has been taken, however," he said through clenched jaws. "Other couriers have been waylaid. I decided it was time to put a stop to it. We have a leak at the Foreign Office, obviously, as our every trip is known in advance. My job was to be stopped, and follow the Frenchies to their master. It won't be another Frenchie, but a traitor in the Foreign Office who is in charge of this plot. There's definitely inside help. I know all our men, and as I've followed the Frenchies this far, I know now where they're heading. The only employee who lives nearby is Sir Herbert Longville. The Frenchies are doubtlessly heading to Longville Manor."

"Heading? They'll be miles ahead of you. They'll be there and gone by now."

"Espionage is not carried out by the broad light of day for everyone to see. They'll sneak in after dark, which is why I've been at pains to stay a little behind them."

This explanation quite took the wind out of my sails. Kestrel's dilatory pace was explained now. He hadn't wanted to overtake the Frenchies, but to remain a discreet distance behind them. It took me a few seconds to discover a flaw in his plan.

"There's no reason to think they'll go to Longville Manor. Sir Herbert is only their London informant. Once they have the information, they'll take it straight along to Boney."

"Not till it's been looked over by Longville, to make sure it's genuine, I think!" Kestrel snapped. "And how do you think they'll get it to France? Longville Manor is right on the coast. Smugglers are the usual means of communication across the Channel. I learned at the Saracen's head a shipment is due to arrive tonight. Even *you* must have realized I had some reason for stopping there."

"But isn't Longville in London?" I asked. Foolish of me.

"No, he goes home every Friday afternoon. This is Friday. He'll be there, and by God, I'll catch the old bleater if it's the last thing I do."

Kestrel appeared less incompetent now that I knew the whole truth. The determined face scowling into the distance looked much more capable than the languorous, bored face I had seen earlier. His riding skill was also enviable.

Ronald was the next one to speak. "The message you were carrying—I take it that was some sort of hoax?" he asked thoughtfully.

"It was genuine. We knew it was someone from the

Foreign Office who was the leak, and he would know if the message was phoney. It was a risk we had to take. Now that you see the importance of my mission, you realize I can't have amateurs getting in my way.''

Amateurs! That was his opinion of our assistance. I opened my lips to object, but before I could speak, Kestrel stepped in. ''Pray spare me the lecture on your dealings with emirs and Arabs, Miss Mathieson. I'm sure you quelled a dozen desert tribes by your own hand, but your knowledge of camels and your few words of Arabic will be of no use in catching Longville. There's too much at stake to have a lady gumming up the works.''

I swallowed my quart of spleen all in one gulp, not to ingratiate this bigheaded jackass, but to learn his plan for trapping Longville. This wasn't the moment to let pride stand in my way. ''What do you plan to do?'' I asked, with a civility that caused me heartburn.

''I plan to stop him, once and for all.''

''Could you be a little more specific? Do you plan to lie in wait for the smugglers to arrive? Or will you find some pretext to actually get into the manor and keep an eye on things from inside? That shouldn't be impossible, as I deduce you are acquainted with Longville. And what about the orders to our army? You said they were genuine orders, and that there was the necessity for speed in delivering them.''

''My groom delivered a copy to Colonel Hackley.''

''I see.'' Once again Kestrel surprised me by having a soupçon of common sense after all. ''About my other questions—where will you go to catch the spies?''

''That need not interest you,'' he said bluntly. ''You've shown a lack of ability to follow orders. I sent you and Kidd south to the coast. You shouldn't be here at all. Pray go to Canterbury. Bore the kipper-crunching crowd there, and leave me free to do my job.'' On this rude speech, he turned and galloped away.

Ronald looked a question at me. "He was a little distraught," I decided, though his words stung like a nettle. Amateur indeed! A "few words of Arabic" and some management of ignorant Bedouins was his assessment of my accomplishments. To add that bit about "boring" my audience was entirely gratuitous. They had been spellbound in London. Tom Moore himself sat mesmerized throughout.

"We might as well go back," Ronald said.

"Go back, and miss out on the exciting part after we've come this far? Ronald, I'm disappointed in you. Naturally we must follow Kestrel and learn what he's up to. Do you trust him to handle Longville by himself? I certainly do not."

"Kestrel is top of the trees, Marion. You may be sure he has some plan. I think it would be best if we just do as he said."

I was beginning to think we were perhaps de trop, but having come this far, I couldn't bear to miss out on the excitement. "When were you upgraded from my secretary to my adviser, Mr. Kidd? I don't recall that promotion. I mean to follow Kestrel. Anything could happen. Of course, if you are afraid of a handful of Frenchies, then you must by all means desert me. You won't forget to look for my lap case at Chatham? I wouldn't want to lose those three chapters of the next Aurelia."

Ronald shook his head. "There's no need to con me. I'll go along, but if we end up getting Kestrel killed and losing the letter to the Frenchies, it's on your shoulders. I officially register my objection here and now."

"Objection duly noted. And when I save Kestrel's life and the letter, will you remember your objection, my good secretary?"

Ronald knew I was only teasing. A "Mr. Kidd" will usually bring him to heel. His mood was just fine as we waited in the road to see which turn Kestrel took.

We would have to keep a considerable distance behind Kestrel, as he looked over his shoulder from time to time to be sure we weren't following. We turned our mounts around as though leaving, but when Kestrel turned right, we weren't far behind him.

A thrill of pleasure trembled up my spine. I hadn't had such fun since the frigate docked in England. I felt a new adventure was stirring, offering the possibility of not only helping my country and gathering material for Aurelia, but of showing Lord Kestrel a much-needed lesson as well. Amateur indeed! Boring my audience!

Chapter Five

The road signs on the corner where Kestrel turned said Dover three miles, Hythe five miles, in the opposite direction. Kestrel did not continue north toward Dover as he had indicated he would, but south toward Hythe. Already the land was taking on the appearance of territory reclaimed from the sea, with Romney Marsh a few miles ahead. That would be an unattractive area populated by a few farms, many sheep, and many bands of smugglers, but where we rode, the coast was still rocky. Some beauty was added by the ocean, visible at times, and always reminding one of its presence by the smell. Kestrel took many a sharp look around to insure he wasn't being followed, which required Ronald and me to be put to the unusual and uncomfortable shift of riding in the ditch, but eventually he turned his mount in at a fine old iron gate. When we reached it a little later, we saw a prosperous private estate. While waiting to stop the first passerby and ascertain that the place was indeed Longville Manor, we laid our plans.

"One of us must have an accident," I said. "Kestrel's an idiot. He's going to waltz straight in and accuse Longville to his face. Much chance he'll have of catching the spies once he's revealed himself. Longville will kill him."

"I can't believe Kestrel would do that. He ain't the

gudgeon we've been thinking," Ronald replied. "In fact, I still think we should go on and leave him in peace."

"In pieces is more like it. He'll need our help before this is over. Are you ready?"

"I take it I'm the one who's going to have an accident? I knew how it would be. I need my cane." He hopped down from his perch and procured himself a stout fallen branch, on which he would hold the weight of his sprained ankle when we went to Sir Herbert's door to seek assistance.

Ronald thought my spraining an ankle would cause greater pity, and a greater chance of being invited to remain to dinner, but I wanted to be free to move about the house. Before going to the door, however, we waited quite half an hour to make sure Kestrel wasn't just making a brief visit. We figured that half an hour at such a time of day (i.e., nearly dinnertime) meant he was remaining to dine. At the appointed time Ronald clambered down from his mount, leaned on the branch and my arm, and I lifted the brass knocker.

The house appeared at first glance to be dismayingly innocent. A country-style butler, well fed and wearing a black jacket, answered the door. He showed no alarm or suspicion at our plight, but with a true Christian kindness invited us into a small waiting parlor, and even offered wine. I peeped around the entrance hall and into the main saloon, but saw no sign of Kestrel or Sir Herbert.

"Would you like me to call a doctor to look at the lad's ankle?" the butler offered.

We hadn't gone so far as to actually sprain Ronald's ankle, so this had to be talked away. We had only rubbed it, to make it red. "It isn't primarily the ankle, really. Mr. Kidd has a weakness of constitution picked up during his travels in the Orient," I explained vaguely. "If he could rest an hour or so, he'll be fine."

"The Orient, eh?" the butler enquired with quick interest.

It was my aim to meet the man of the house, and I hoped my reputation might fulfill that aim. "Yes, I am Miss Mathieson," I replied, looking from the corner of my eye to see if he recognized the name.

"From India, are you?" he asked. This told me my fame had not spread to the provinces. Oates was wise to have arranged the lecture tour.

"No, the Orient."

While the butler stood smiling, there was the sound of light footfalls at the doorway, and a young lady came into the room. She appeared as innocent and provincial as the rest of the house. She was a pretty enough girl, with brown hair and dark eyes. Her gown, I suspected, was local in origin, and her coiffure nonexistent. Her hair just sat on her head, curled but not arranged.

Ronald hopped to his feet with an alacrity that belied a sprained ankle. A sharp squeeze on the derrière caused a good, convincing wince. I noticed he looked with favor on the young provincial, and she displayed an equal interest in him. "Ronald, you'd best sit down," I reminded him.

I offered the girl my hand. "I am Miss Mathieson, and this is my secretary, Mr. Kidd."

"Miss Longville," she replied, smiling, but not with the smile that hinted at recognition.

"My secretary had a dizzy spell on the road beyond your place, and fell from his mount. I fear he has twisted his ankle. I hope you will excuse our encroaching manners, Miss Longville, but the only thing for these dizzy spells is a short period of lying down."

She turned to the butler. "You may leave us, Ruggers," she said. As soon as the butler left, she returned her gaze to Ronald. It was a brightly curious, anticipatory look. Ronald is not the most handsome man in the world, but with a provincial I daresay he might cause a favorable impression. "What has been done with your mount and your personal things?" she enquired.

"We left our mounts tethered out front," he answered.

"I'll see to them."

She swept from the room, leaving us to wonder what she had in mind. Was she going to have the nags stabled? Why not ask the butler to do it? "Country manners," I explained to Ronald.

"She's beautiful, isn't she?" he said, smiling fondly at the door.

"She's not an antidote. I wonder where Kestrel is, and Sir Herbert. I think you must have a fainting spell when she returns, Ronald. If we can get you into a bed, we'll be here for an hour at least. I hope she offers us dinner. Won't Kestrel stare to see me sitting across from him!"

"They'll all stare if you plan to go to the table in that dusty traveling suit."

"Bother! One forgets the restrictions of English society. I hope Miss Longville has something I can fit into. She's such a little squab, her gowns will be above my ankles. And these vulgar red slippers! They're comfortable, though."

"She's dainty as a sylph," Ronald smiled.

"Dainty as two sylphs rolled together. Her body is fuller than mine. It's the length I'm concerned about."

The well-rounded sylph returned wearing a frown of confusion. "You don't have any cases. There was nothing but the mounts."

"We were just out for a ride," I answered swiftly, before Ronald took into his noggin to say more than he should. "We are visiting at Dover, and wanted to see a bit of the countryside while we're here."

"Would you like to send a message to someone?" Miss Longville asked.

"No, we are putting up at a hotel."

Miss Longville raised a prudish eyebrow at this. "Mr. Kidd is my nephew," I assured her, "as well as my secretary."

"It is odd, a lady having a secretary," she said.

"I am an author. Perhaps you've heard of my book, *A Gentlewoman's Memoirs of the Orient*? I was to lecture at Canterbury tonight, but had to postpone it."

Her "Oh" said as plain as day she'd never heard of me, and had very little interest in the Orient besides. A herd of sheep would be of more interest to this country bumpkin. As the girl was rather simple, I had to remind her of the patient. "Would it be possible for Mr. Kidd to lie down somewhere for an hour or so?"

"He can stay right here," she answered witlessly, pointing to the sofa he sat on.

"Perhaps we'd best send for a doctor after all. He's passing out," I announced, with a commanding eye to Ronald, who promptly fell into a marvelous coma.

"I hope it's not contagious!" Miss Longville said, and jumped back a yard or two.

With great forbearance, I didn't box her ears. "Call your Ruggers and a couple of footmen. We must get him into bed at once. He'll require plenty of covers and some hot soup. It isn't contagious, Miss Longville. It is like intelligence in that respect."

"But what ails him?"

"It is a fever of the brain."

"Oh dear! I don't know what Papa will say!"

This was the first interesting utterance to have left her lips. "Your papa dislikes company, does he?" I asked. This seemed the expected behavior of a traitorous spy.

"It's not that. He already has company. Lord Kestrel is staying with us overnight."

"Overnight!"

Strangely, the witless thing picked up on my peculiar reaction, mentioning the length of Kestrel's visit. There was a somewhat knowing look in her eyes as she examined me. She didn't say anything, but there was definitely a knowing look in her eyes. "I'll call Ruggers," she said, and left.

Ronald recovered sufficiently to walk upstairs on Ruggers's arm. I went up behind him, accompanied by Miss Longville. "We are about to have dinner, Miss Mathieson," she said. "Could you be prevailed upon to join us?"

"If you have a gown I could borrow, I should be delighted," I answered.

"Come to my room while they settle Mr. Kidd in. We can be alone there."

One hardly expected to change in front of men, but I found her "alone" rather ominous. When we were alone, she said, "Did you know Lord Kestrel was here?" A sharp look in her eyes caused me a moment's consternation, till I figured out she thought I was throwing my hankie at him and had come here haring after him.

This put me in the devil of a predicament. I wanted to deny any knowledge of the man, but what if Kestrel blurted out that he did know me? It seemed more likely he would not do this, however, so I said, "Lord Kestrel?" in a confused sort of way that left the door open to recognition later if necessary.

"He works with my father at Whitehall, and lives nearby."

"It is strange he stays overnight then."

"He plans to return to London tomorrow morning. Something has come up."

"I see. I hope there isn't any trouble."

"No, just some government business."

She opened the door of her clothespress to reveal a smarter collection of gowns than I anticipated. A few compliments brought forth a smile.

"I live in London. I'm my father's hostess there,"

she said. "I don't dress up at home. Papa says it puts the constituents off for me to dress too grandly. If I'd known Kestrel was coming . . ."

"How about this one?" I said, selecting a dashing blue crepe gown, cut to the latest fashion. "Do I have time to bathe? I'm covered in dust from our ride."

"Dinner is nearly ready. You'll have to make do with a quick washup."

She called for a basin of hot water and left me alone to tend to my toilette. While I washed, brushed my hair into a basket of curls, and donned the pretty blue gown, I could hardly contain my mirth to think of Kestrel's shock when he saw me. The fit of the gown was far from perfect, being too loose and to short, but it was passable. I had more important worries than the fit of a gown. I must speak first when Kestrel was introduced, to let him know we two were strangers. When I was prepared, I went into the hall and saw Miss Longville just coming from Ronald's room. She wore a frown.

"How is he?" I enquired, with all the solicitude of a mother hen for her brood.

"He seems fine."

"Then I shan't look in till after dinner. I have delayed you too long already." Ronald couldn't have heard her say Kestrel was remaining overnight, or he would be less than fine. These brain fevers are obliging. He would have a relapse after dinner.

Kestrel's reaction was all I could wish for. He would have had me excommunicated on the spot if he could. He nearly choked on his sherry when I entered the saloon with Miss Longville, while I was as calm under fire as a diplomat telling lies. When he recovered, he wore the stiff face of a stranger.

"This must be Lord Kestrel," I smiled, and went to shake Sir Herbert's hand.

"That is my father, Sir Herbert," Miss Longville told me.

"Delighted to meet you, Sir Herbert," I said, and sized him up swiftly as we exchanged a few pleasantries. He wore the disguise of a country squire whose main interest was his herd of sheep. Working at Whitehall was mere duty, to judge by his conversation, but he didn't fool me for a minute. His blue eyes were as sharp as needles.

"And this must be Lord Kestrel," I said, when Miss Longville took me along to meet him. "Now that I see you more closely, I see you aren't quite old enough to be Miss Longville's papa, unless you had married quite young," I told him artlessly.

Kestrel bowed briefly. "Miss Mathieson" is all he said. Not even "Happy to make your acquaintance."

Miss Longville latched herself on to Kestrel's arm and led him to a sofa to finish the sherry before dinner, which left me with Sir Herbert.

"Your daughter tells me your work at Whitehall," I said leadingly.

"A man must do what he can during these troubled times. When we get Boney put away, I'll come back and get on with my real work. Are you interested in sheep at all, Miss Mathieson?"

"I am interested in everything," I said, planning to revert to Boney at the first opportunity. No such opportunity arose during the whole time I was alone with him. What we discussed, by which I mean he spoke and I listened, was his plan to cross his own Romney rams with some Rambouillet ewes he hoped to get his hands on after the war. To hear him talk, his sole interest in the war was to get hold of those Rambouillets. It seemed this French sheep was a fine-wool animal, whereas his Romneys were long, coarse wool. Why these two breeds should be crossed was of no interest to me, nor you either, I daresay.

Not till we sat around the table did any other matter than sheep come up. Naturally, the meal was lamb, but welcome for all that. Before Sir Herbert could start telling us what breed we were eating, I spoke up. "Miss Longville tells me you work with her papa at Whitehall, Lord Kestrel," I said, and smiled innocently across the table.

He gave me a look that went through me like a knife and replied, "That's right. Excellent lamb, Sir Herbert. Your own?"

For five minutes there was no talk worth listening to. I have attended spinsters' wakes that were livelier than that dinner party. I eased back to Boney via the back door. "When do you think we will see the last of Bonaparte, and you can get those Rambouillet rams, Sir Herbert?"

"Ewes, madam. I have rams aplenty. These are troubled times," he said sadly. "The whole coast feels as if it were under siege, with only the Channel between us and Boney. I hope he don't come during the week, while I am in London. My steward has his orders, but I would prefer to be here myself. I'm afraid of damage to my flock." He was as cunning at returning to his sheep as I at avoiding them.

"What you ought to do is leave your daughter at home, Sir Herbert," Kestrel suggested, with an admiring glance at the provincial.

"Nel is too valuable to me in London. I need a hostess since my good lady passed away." Nel scowled at her papa. Was it possible the provincial would have preferred being buried in the country? "She's better off where I can keep an eye on her," he added.

"You can't expect your daughter to fill that role for long. Some young fellow will steal her away from you," Kestrel warned. Again his eyes lingered on Miss Longville, who glared at her father. Sir Herbert's words and her reaction hinted at a liaison that had the father's disapproval.

I turned a curious glance toward the blushing beauty

70

and said, "Are you satisfied with such a paltry role in life, Miss Longville? I would not be satisfied arranging dinner parties after spending the last few years much more interestingly. My nephew and I are just returned from the Orient, Sir Herbert," I said.

"Ah yes. Our Karakul comes from there. A beautiful tight fur, if you skin them at a young age, but the meat is tough, I believe."

"They cook the meat over an open fire, and it is excellent," I replied, undaunted. "Of course, most foods are cooked over an open fire. In the mountains of Lebanon, they actually eat the flesh raw. Just skin the animal and eat it."

"That sounds mighty unappealing to me," Sir Herbert scowled.

"I daresay one gets accustomed to anything. Riding camels, living in a tent. Mind you, some of the tents are quite lovely, and very comfortable. I had one lined with satin."

"Living in a tent sounds horrid!" Miss Longville frowned. "You must have suffered great deprivations, Miss Mathieson."

"Great deprivation, and yet at times, more luxury than you can imagine. I shall never forget entering Pasha Suliman's marble palace, to find him reclining on a crimson sofa, surrounded by hundreds of guards, all with their swords drawn. That whole trip glows in my memory. It was at the time of the Ramadan, that is, the ninth month of the Mohammedan year, of course, which is holy for them. The whole city ablaze with lights at night, and in the bazaars some of the people poured coffee on the ground before me."

"Whatever for?" Miss Longville enquired.

"Why, it is a mark of respect!"

"It sounds more like an insult to me! Why, it might have destroyed your gown."

Kestrel's eyelids drooped lazily. "Miss Mathieson

71

obviously speaks ex cathedra on oriental matters, Miss Longville. Did you wear gowns in the desert, Miss Mathieson?''

Miss Longville snickered into her fist at the image of me in my petticoats. I didn't take up Kestrel's childish challenge, but went on to tell them a few of my more outstanding memories. When the dessert arrived, I realized I had run on longer than I intended. ''But I don't want to bore you,'' I said, with an arch glance to Kestrel, who couldn't have looked more bored had he tried. His eyelids were nearly closed. He didn't want me upsetting the torpor of that somnolent party.

''It saves us a trip to hear your lecture,'' he said. ''Miss Mathieson gives lectures on her experiences abroad,'' he added to Miss Longville, who hadn't even the normal curiosity to enquire where, or when. ''I saw her posters in London.''

''I shall not be lecturing in Hythe,'' I said. ''If you are interested in the matter, my book is probably available here. It is called *A Gentlewoman's Memoirs of the Orient*.''

''A bargain at ten shillings,'' Lord Kestrel added, but his look suggested the bargain was in not having to listen to me. I really hadn't planned to run on quite so long.

After dessert, we ladies retired and left the gentlemen to their port. I longed to stay behind, but Miss Longville reminded me that I was to look in on Ronald. She went upstairs with me, which made any interesting conversation impossible.

''My, you do look peaked!'' I exclaimed when I entered Ronald's room, and went on to give him a hint he must quit improving. ''You'll end up having to remain overnight like Lord Kestrel if we aren't careful.''

He caught on at once, and sighed wearily against the pillows. Miss Longville looked at his empty tray, betraying a sound appetite not usually associated with invalids. "You've gone and eaten red meat, Ronald," I scolded. "You know you shouldn't when you're having one of your attacks."

"Shall I send for a doctor?" our hostess enquired.

"English doctors have very little notion how to treat Ronald's ailment. In the Orient they have a herbal remedy. Lacking that, rest is the best thing."

"Then you must stay overnight," Miss Longville offered, not with alacrity or joy, but grudgingly.

She sat down to wait till the gentlemen were through with their port. She struck me as the sort of girl who preferred the company of men to ladies. Her conversation was all directed to Ronald. "Miss Mathieson has been entertaining us with tales of your travels," she said. "It sounds very exciting."

"We've had a few interesting experiences," he allowed modestly. "In fact, from the moment we were shipwrecked off Rhodes and had to spend the night in a cave, the last three years have been an unending variety of novelty. I think the most hair-raising experience we had was the time of our visit to Palmyra. We had to befriend all the tribes—Ishmael Aga, chief of the Delibash, and Mohanna el Fadel, chief of all the Anizi tribes. Bribed them all, and still our guides deserted us in the middle of the desert. Prince Nasar, Mohanna's son, was the scoundrel who turned coat on us."

Miss Longville showed enough interest that he continued for a generous length of time with tales of pashas and sheikhs, till I began to see that one could get too much of that sort of thing. I would curb my reminiscences in future. Ronald's ranting sounded a good deal like showing off to the provincial. When Miss Longville figured Kestrel was free, she excused herself and went below. I stayed behind with Ronald for a moment.

"Throwing your bonnet at the shepherdess, are you?" I teased.

"She's lovely, isn't she?"

"Charming, but Kestrel is running you a close race. You noticed how she hotfooted it out of here when she thought he would be free?"

Ronald gave me a sly smile and changed the topic. "How was dinner?"

"A perfect nightmare of boredom."

"What opinion did you pick up of Sir Herbert?"

"He's as big a rogue as Prince Nasar. You'd think to hear him he hadn't a thing on his mind but sheep. He doesn't reveal a word of his real activities. I must find an opportunity to get Kestrel in private and see what he plans to do. Kestrel, I fear, isn't on to his curves."

"If you can get him away from Miss Longville, that is."

So that was the meaning behind his sly smile! Ronald thought I had Kestrel in mind as a flirt for myself. "You should know me better, after all these years."

"Oh, I know you'll detach him from her and have him around your thumb eventually, but he don't wind as easily as most, does he?"

"Pokers don't wind at all, and that is not what I meant! She is welcome to Kestrel."

Ronald didn't continue this pointless subject, but resumed business. "I have a view of the rear of the estate and the stables from my window. I kept a watch during dinner, but didn't see anyone come."

"No matter if they had come. Sir Herbert wasn't out of our sight for a moment, and Kestrel is with him now. When we must be on guard is after the family retire. It will be early—it's that sort of establishment. After I return below, Ronald, you have a look around upstairs and find Sir Herbert's bedchamber. If the coast is clear, go in and have a look for clues. If you're caught, say your headache is killing you, and you were looking for a headache powder. Lay it on thick, mind. We don't want them suspecting. Sir Herbert's servants might be in on it as well."

"What do you think I've been doing the past hour? I've found Sir Herbert's chamber. There was nothing in it but his estate accounts and a pile of books about sheep."

"He hides his activities behind sheep. A wolf in sheep's clothing is what he is. The more interesting things must be in his office downstairs. I'll try my hand at it later tonight. Now I must go. Keep an eye on the rear window."

I darted out, back downstairs to rejoin the dull little party, which I would not enliven with one word about any place east of Dover, not if they all fell asleep in their chairs.

Chapter Six

When I returned below, the room looked as though Madame Tussaud had brought her traveling wax museum to call. Three inert figures sat on chairs, staring dumbly into the distance. Kestrel would have run out and hung himself had he realized what an expression of relief descended on his features.

"Ah, here is Miss Mathieson!" he exclaimed joyfully. "How is your secretary, Miss Mathieson? Feeling a little better, I hope?"

"About the same, I fear. He is suffering from a fever contracted—" I came to a screaming halt. Not one word of the East! "Contracted a while ago," I concluded.

Kestrel eased into a smile. "Something he picked up in the desert, is it?"

"Very likely."

Sir Herbert came to life and picked up a magazine. Miss Longville stared at us, mute as a picture on the wall, then strolled to the window, where she seemed wrapped up in thought.

Kestrel moved closer on the sofa for some private conversation. We had to keep our voices low because of Sir Herbert. "Did you ever come across this paralysis of the tongue during your travels?" he asked.

"No, sir. This, if I am not mistaken, is a peculiarly

English provincial disease. Possibly contracted from too close an association with sheep.''

"There is something positive to be said about shrews after all. At least they don't hesitate to use their tongues.''

"As you so kindly imply, mine has never suffered from lack of exercise. I would like an opportunity to talk to you in private, if possible.'' This time Kestrel didn't look as though I meant to throw myself on his neck and make an improper proposal, as he did at the hop-picker's cottage. Instead he glanced to see if anyone would notice our departure. Before we could get away, the door knocker sounded. We both jumped to rigid attention, ready for trouble.

The new addition to the party certainly didn't look dangerous. He was introduced as Mr. Harcourt, a neighbor, and he proved to be a younger version of Sir Herbert—already portly at twenty-six or seven, red of face, boring of conversation, unstylish in toilette. Before long, he turned a yearning eye in Miss Longville's direction. The papa obviously approved the match, as he suggested Nel, the name he called his daughter, show Alfred the new *Sheepbreeders' Monthly* that had apparently arrived that day in the post. "An excellent article on sheeprot,'' he added as further inducement to romance. Not that Alfred needed it.

With a mutinous scowl, Nel lumbered to the table where the magazine was kept. She had an ungainly walk for a lady. Mr. Harcourt went after her, and they took up seats apart from the rest of us. Sir Herbert turned to me. "Your nevvie is still poorly, you say?''

"His fever is still bothering him. Your daughter was kind enough to ask us to remain overnight.'' I didn't risk a glance at Kestrel, but from the corner of my eye I saw his head slew toward me.

"There is plenty of room. We're happy to have you,'' Longville said.

"If you gentlemen have business to discuss, pray don't dally on my account," I offered. My aim was to get out of the room and do some searching around the house and grounds.

Sir Herbert showed interest in escape, but he didn't seem to think Kestrel was necessary for his business. "I do have a few letters I ought to get out tonight. If you two can amuse each other for an hour, I will join you then for a nightcap."

Kestrel bowed his acquiescence, I smiled mine, and Sir Herbert lumbered off. I saw where Nel had inherited her gait. The man had scarcely left the room when Kestrel took my arm and led me off a little from the lovers in the corner, courting to the subject of sheeprot. We stood near the door, out of sight of the courting couple.

"You haven't explained to me what you're doing here," he said.

"I *did* explain. Ronald has a fever."

"He'll have a cracked skull when I get hold of him. I told you I wanted to handle this myself."

"A gentleman should accept defeat more gracefully, Lord Kestrel. We are here, and we shall stay for as long as necessary. Frankly, I think it imprudent of you to have come barging in as you did at this time with no apparent reason. Sir Herbert is bound to suspect something."

"Give me credit for some sense. I didn't come barging in with no reason. I took the precaution of having a message to deliver from the Foreign Office."

"He'll wonder why the French spies didn't relieve you of that while they stole the other letter."

"He doesn't know I was held up."

"Of course he knows! He's the one who tipped them off the letter was en route."

Kestrel shook his head doubtfully. "I didn't say I had a letter to deliver to Longville—I said a message. It was a verbal message, as we didn't know when I left London who would be the recipient. After some careful consideration, I don't think Sir Herbert does know about the holdup. You can see for yourself he isn't the sort to be playing at spy games. I begin to think I've made a gross error here. The man's life is this sheepfarm. His family have been here for centuries. And his place is quite prosperous. A man like that doesn't betray his country.''

''It's those damned Rambouillet rams he's after.''

''Ewes! Odd you can't remember that.''

''I don't fill my head with useless trivia. Rams, ewes, what's the difference, except to other sheep?''

''It makes a difference to us sheepbreeders.''

''You! Don't tell me you're another mutton man!'' This struck me as so ludicrous that a spontaneous laugh escaped my lips. I pictured all sheepbreeders as being similar to Sir Herbert and Mr. Harcourt—country bumpkins. I could no more picture Kestrel raising sheep than I could picture him catching the spies without my help. Kestrel went into a pucker, and I felt the judicious course was to add sheep to the list of forbidden topics. ''I mistook you for a city buck.''

''I expect that is a backhanded compliment,'' he decided.

''Before your head begins swelling, I must point out I don't agree with your reasoning about Sir Herbert. This sheep thing is a ruse to divert suspicion. No one could be that preoccupied with dumb animals. I believe he is an extremely cunning traitor. The question is, how do we set about proving it? Ronald has searched his bedchamber, with no success. What we must do is get into his study this evening after he retires.''

''I still don't believe it, but as the spies were headed in this direction, and as there's no one else at the F.O. living near here, I must complete my investigation. Alone,'' he added, with a commanding stare.

''It might be best if we work independently,'' I

agreed. "They say two heads are better than one, and I daresay that means the two heads aren't stuck together, like the shepherdess and her shepherd there." I looked toward the corner as I spoke, and noticed that the two heads were, in fact, not together at all. Alfred's was stuck in the *Sheepbreeders' Monthly*, while Miss Longville's was turned in our direction, looking as if she would like to join us.

"Alfred won't win her, carrying on in that fashion," Kestrel said.

"Is he a suitor?"

"Sir Herbert favors him—rather too strongly, in my opinion. He's given his consent, without Nel's approval. That's bound to create mischief."

"Why did he do such a thing?"

"She has a handsome young wastrel in her eye. A local fellow named Bernard Kemp. If it weren't for some good connections on his mother's side, he wouldn't be allowed into respectable houses. He's run through his own fortune and is looking about for another one to marry. Miss Longville is extremely eligible. That is why her father takes her to London."

"And Mr. Harcourt?"

"Likewise. Their farms march together. It would be an excellent match so far as real estate goes."

"Good God, I never heard anything so gothic in my life!"

A satirical eyebrow lifted in my direction. "It's by no means unusual. I made sure you would have a string of eastern customs to top it. Brides bartered for camels . . ." A quizzing smile egged me on to make a fool of myself again.

I was still embarrassed about my tirade over dinner, especially after mentally chastising Ronald for the same thing. "I was merely trying to find something other than sheep to discuss at dinner. I daresay I ran on longer than anyone enjoyed."

Kestrel was well-bred enough to apologize for his jibes. "I, for one, enjoyed it, my behavior to the contrary. Any little shots of irony were mere ill humor at discovering you had worked your way in here against my wishes. Or perhaps it was your mistaking me for Nel's father that got my feathers ruffled. I come to see you are a lady who doesn't take anything sitting down. We have that in common, you know," he warned, with a gleam of amusement darting out from beneath his drooping eyelids.

"Then it seems we are at an impasse. You don't want my assistance; I have every intention of forcing it on you. One of us immovable objects of stubbornness should be watching for the arrival of the spies. Sir Herbert cannot have met with them yet. Unless— Good gracious, Kestrel, he could be meeting with them right now while we stand here twiddling our thumbs!"

He shook his head, peering toward the door. "No one's entered his study. I've kept an eye peeled. Why do you think we're standing uncomfortably behind a sofa, instead of sitting on it?"

"The spies might have been in there waiting for him. Or there could be a secret passage. This isn't good enough. You must go and investigate. Pretend you want to talk to him."

"I? I'm honored that you place the duty on my shoulders."

"It would seem more natural coming from you."

"Very true; I know the difference between a ram and a ewe. I'll go and cadge a drink from him."

He walked off, and I lent an ear to the lovers in the corner. Alfred's wheedling voice was low, but audible. "Why not, Nel?" he begged. "You know your papa will make you have me in the end. I've put a new carpet in the saloon—blue, just as you like."

"Papa needs me," she replied firmly. "While he still works at Whitehall, I cannot abandon him."

"He's said a dozen times his sister would go to London with him. You have a beau there, haven't you?" he asked jealously.

Miss Longville lifted her square chin and looked away, not deigning to answer. As she turned her head toward me, I quickly looked in another direction. I happened to spot a carafe of wine and some glasses on the sofa table. Kestrel's excuse for interrupting Sir Herbert was ill chosen, but it gave me something to do till he returned. I poured myself a glass of wine and sat down. Within a minute Kestrel was back, carrying a glass in his hand. He joined me on the sofa.

I pointed to the wine. "Next time, choose your excuse more carefully. There's wine here."

"Wine? Oh, I was after brandy."

"Is that what you're drinking! Kestrel, you know where brandy comes from! It's smuggled in from France. If Sir Herbert has brandy—well, it's perfectly obvious he's in league with the smugglers. They bring him brandy, and he ships out secret documents. Imagine his being stupid enough to offer you brandy."

I expected surprise, perhaps a word of praise for my deducing. It was no such a thing. Kestrel's lip curled in derision. "If having a keg of brandy in the cellar were enough to condemn a man, there wouldn't be a pair of trousers in all of Kent walking free, including my own."

"Do you mean to sit there and tell me you actually contribute to the French economy at a time like this? Putting money in Boney's coffers to buy cannons?"

"No, money in our own English smugglers' hands. And before you point a finger, I might just remind you that the silk in that pretty gown you're wearing also comes illegally from France."

If he thought to gain a point there, he was badly mistaken. "Of course it does! It belongs to Miss Longville."

He looked with some interest at the gown. "I thought

it was not quite in your style," he said. The gown, you recall, had been described as "pretty." I noticed when he said it that a compliment sounded out of place on his lips. Determined not to show my pique, I changed the subject.

"What was Sir Herbert doing when you saw him? Was he alone?"

"Just he and his ink pot. He was writing to Sussex to purchase some sheep-dip. Our own Kent supplier is better, but Sir Herbert is an experimenter."

"He won't meet the spies till we all retire. I believe I'll do it now and save myself a lecture on sheep-dip."

A mocking smile raked my face, lingering while Kestrel thought of a clever retort for my insulting the sheep-breeders. "Lectures on subject matter foreign to the listener *do* tend to become tedious," he said blandly.

"I haven't mentioned the East since I came back downstairs!"

"I noticed it, and I am extremely grateful for you forbearance, Miss Mathieson."

"You *said* you enjoyed it!" You may imagine with what a chilly air I took my leave of him. I stopped to say good night to the couple in the corner as well. Alfred stumbled to his feet and bowed. Miss Longville said she hoped I slept well. I told her I was extremely fatigued, to prevent her stopping at my room later, and I left. Nothing had been settled about searching Sir Herbert's office, but I fully intended to do it, whatever about Kestrel. I stopped off to see Ronald. He had his lights out and his window open, with his head stuck out to hear what went on, as vision was poor.

"What's afoot?" I enquired.

"It's silent as a tomb out there."

"I have officially retired for the night. I'm going to go out and scout around."

"I'll go with you."

"No, you'd best stay here in case someone decides

to check up on your fever. If you hear anyone approach my door, tell them I don't want to be disturbed.''

"What if it's Kestrel?''

I gave him an icy stare, invisible, of course, in the dark room, but my tone was also frosty. "I shouldn't think it at all likely he would do anything of the sort.''

"But if he does?''

"Oh, for heaven's sake, Ronald! Use your head. You can tell *him* what I'm doing.''

Ronald gave an arch laugh. "That's what I thought,'' he answered.

Not knowing what I might end up doing outdoors, I deemed it wise to change back into my own traveling suit. It would be difficult to explain a rent or grass strain on her "pretty'' gown to Miss Longville. To prevent the possibility of being seen if I went out by a door, I opened my bedroom window and let myself down by a thick branch of ivy that clung to the wall of the house. Not a word will I write about having had more perilous escapes abroad. The trip made tatters of my gloves, but they were already beyond polite use. Once on the ground, I took my bearings before doing anything else.

It was a chilly night. The soughing of the wind in the branches was strong enough to be heard above the breaking of the waves at the shore beyond sight. The sky was covered in layers of long, ragged clouds. If there was a moon, it was invisible, but a lightening at the edge of some of the clouds suggested it was up there, trying to shine. My bedroom was at the back of the house, looking toward barns and outbuildings. It was possible Sir Herbert would come out this way later, but at the moment there was no sign of life, and I didn't intend to enter that cavernous, black barn alone. What I wished to investigate first was what Sir Herbert was up to, and with that in mind, I skirted the house to his office. His drapes were partially drawn, but by standing on my tiptoes I had a view of him. He still sat at his desk, scribbling away. From time to time he looked at a magazine, or checked some address in a book by his side. What was he writing there, looking as innocent as the sheepfarmer he pretended to be?

I looked sharply for a long letter bearing a seal, which would indicate he had already got the letter stolen from Kestrel by the Frenchies. Nothing of the sort was seen. A little later, Mr. Harcourt stuck his head in at the door, smiled, said a few words, and left. Was Harcourt in on this nefarious business with Longville? It was possible. I nipped around to the front of the house, waiting for Harcourt to come out. He didn't, but not much later I heard the sound of hoofbeats and the jingle of a harness, and saw Harcourt cutting across a field from the direction of the barn. Naturally, he had stabled his mount when he came calling. I knew no letter had been passed to Harcourt for delivery, so I forgot about him and returned to Sir Herbert's window.

Miss Longville was with her father now. She wore her mulish face, Sir Herbert one of frustration. His arms flailed and his lips moved angrily. Whatever he said threw Nel into a fit of tears. She pulled out a handkerchief, raised it to her eyes. Then she lowered it, said something in a bold way, stamped her foot, and stalked from the office. Sir Herbert mumbled and poured himself another glass of smuggled brandy. It wouldn't take a genius to realize the father had been urging her to marry Harcourt. Poor girl, I could feel sympathy for her predicament. How perfectly wretched to be shackled to a dull sheepfarmer for life, especially after a taste of London excitement. If time allowed, I might try to help her after we caught the traitor. In fact, I doubted Harcourt would be so eager to have her once her papa was revealed for the villain he was. They do say every cloud has a silver lining.

Sir Herbert was an extremely uninteresting villain, insofar as his activities that night went. He wrote another letter, put out his lamp, and left the office. If he was going to meet with the spies, this was the time for it. I rather thought Kestrel might join me, preferably with his pistol in his hand. I crept back to keep an eye on the barn and the rear of the house, for it seemed unlikely spies would enter by the front door. For fifteen minutes I skulked in the shadows, feeling quite cold and uncomfortable. Not a single thing happened. There wasn't even an owl or night creature stirring. I decided to make a circuit of the house, and went softly around the corner, back toward Sir Herbert's office. I hardly bothered to glance at it, but my eye was caught by a flicker of light. Not a lamp, but a smaller light, moving freely through the room.

My heart thumped with excitement as I approached the window and put my nose to the pane. There was someone searching the office! A spy had come to get the stolen letter. Sir Herbert had secreted it in some prearranged spot. Probably all his scribbling was intended for Boney's eyes as well. I was in a fever to let Kestrel know. He was the one who had the pistol, and a pistol would be required to catch this spy. The candle was raised, held at arm's length. The flame was so weak I couldn't get a clear view of the man holding it. Not till he put it on the table and riffled through Sir Herbert's correspondence could I make out the black slash of brows, the arrogant nose, and square chin of Lord Kestrel. He had taken my hint and gone to search Sir Herbert's office after all. I was a little piqued that he hadn't asked me to help him, or at least stand guard. I thought of tapping on the window and giving him a fright, but decided against it. He wasn't having any luck in the office, so why should I waste time on him?

What I really wanted to do was to catch Sir Herbert and the spies myself, to hand them over to Kestrel on a platter to repay him for his various slights. He thought I was a boaster, a claimer of accomplishments not my own. I'd show him. But how? The spies weren't here, and even if they were, I had no weapon to stop them. The logical thing to do was to arm myself, and this meant entering the house again and finding where Longville kept his weapons. I thought of that rough branch of ivy and the steep crawl up to my room. Perhaps there was a door left open somewhere. But lights still burned in the kitchen, where the servants would be at work cleaning the dishes and setting out the morning's bread.

I took one more look through Sir Herbert's window, where Kestrel was just leaving, his candle still in his hand. He closed the door, and the room became invisible. The downstairs was in darkness now, save for the kitchen area. I had seen a French door at the far side of the house, leading to a hedged garden. Perhaps that door was off the latch. Back I went, peering into the shadows beyond, where nothing stirred but the wind in the leaves. I edged up to the door, put a hand out, and gently tried the knob. To my surprise and delight, it turned silently under my fingers. Did country folks leave their doors off the latch when they retired, or was this one left open on purpose to welcome a spy? I didn't think Sir Herbert could be back downstairs yet, or Kestrel wouldn't be moving about so freely. I eased the door open and stepped into utter darkness.

I closed the door behind me and stood a moment getting my bearings. What room would this be, and where situated in the house? More important, were there any weapons in the room? What I needed was a light. I took a few tentative steps, feeling around me for a table, hopefully holding a tinderbox and lamp. I thought I heard a sound, and stopped, ears cocked. If someone was coming, I must flee out the door. But the sound, if indeed there was a sound, wasn't repeated. My fingers felt a sharp edge of wood. It was long, flat—a table or desk. I carefully moved my hand over it, hoping to feel the tinderbox.

Then I stopped, my heart hammering against my ribs. I definitely had heard a sound! A very soft, secretive sound, as of a foot moving carefully over a carpet. I felt an intuition so strong, it amounted to certainty that there was someone in the room. I held my breath, trying to decide what to do. Unarmed as I was, escape seemed the best choice. Yet escape, if I was followed, would mean leaving the safety of a house for the danger of the outdoors. Sir Herbert—who else could it be?— would hardly put a bullet through me in his own house, where the sound would be heard by everyone. If only I knew where the door to the hallway was located! The sound came again—soft, a mere susurrus, a muted rustling as of pieces of clothing rubbing together. A jacket sleeve against a jacket, or trouser legs . . .

For a split second common sense deserted me and instinct took precedence. I turned and bolted for the one door whose location I knew. I wanted only to escape—whether into greater peril outdoors didn't matter. I had lost my bearings and bumped into the table. That moment's delay brought my attacker down on me. A heavy blow struck my head, just above the left eye. I was hit so hard, a hollow echo reverberated in the room. It was the last thing I heard before the ringing started in my ears, and I fell into merciful oblivion.

Chapter Seven

As I lay on the floor with my poor head pounding and reeling, I was dimly aware of other things going forth in the room. There was the sound of furtive footsteps hastening toward the door in the hallway. The door closed, and there was a scuffling outside it. My poor, addled wits deduced that Kestrel had been lurking nearby and caught my assailant as he left the room. I tried to sit up, and felt such a stab of pain in my temple, I let out a moan, then passed out stone-cold. The next time I was aware of anything I was on a sofa, propped up with pillows, covered with a crocheted throw, with a glass of something vile pressed to my lips. A man hovered above me, one of his arms holding me up to drink. He was trying to poison me! I raised a hand and batted the awful-tasting stuff away.

An educated curse rent the air, and peering through the dim shadow, I recognized the features of Lord Kestrel, glaring at me like a hawk. "Oh, it's you!" I exclaimed, and felt foolish for my forceful spurning of his help. Being held in his arms did nothing to help me recover my sangfroid. Though I have had many adventures and experiences, my amorous doings and Aurelia's all came from the realm of fantasy. I really felt extraordinarily uncomfortable with a man's arms around me. And to make it worse, I realized that the shadow in his eyes wasn't anger, but alarm, or fear for my safety. "I thought someone was trying to poison me. What was that awful liquid?" I asked, to cover my *gêne*. I knew perfectly well I was blushing like a green cow, and hoped he would mistake it for the effect of the brandy. I realized now the burning liquor was that.

The glare softened to a reluctant smile. At this close range, I noticed Kestrel's lashes were very long. They were what gave his eyes that penetrating look—the pale gray eyes were emphasized by the dark outline. With a smile curving his lips, he appeared more attractive than before, and the embarrassment of being in his arms was intensified accordingly. "Brandy," he said. "Are you all right, Marion?"

I couldn't control my eyes at that "Marion," which slipped out unawares. "Other than a splitting headache and a suit now decorated with brandy as well as mud and dust, I seem to be intact," I said breathlessly.

He returned my head to the pillows, but with one arm still around me, which had the effect of drawing his broad shoulders in an arch around me. I remembered how he had looked that morning with his jacket off. At this close range, actually touching in places, I could feel his body heat. Belvoir's "hard wall" of chest that comforted Aurelia in times of strife had been woefully inadequate. A man's chest wasn't like a wall, cold and impersonal. There was animal warmth, comfort. The lips were very close when a man had his arms around you. Close enough to touch. With his other hand, Kestrel reached out and brushed the hair from my forehead. "You're going to have a bruise there," he said. His breaths fanned my cheek, heightening the unfamiliar excitement of intimacy. His voice was tender—for Kestrel, I mean.

My forehead was tender, too. I winced and moved my head aside. "Tell me, is there a lamp in this room?

It seems a little brighter than before, but I don't see any lamp."

"I have a candle here on the floor," he answered. "I didn't want to light the lamps and draw attention, but I had to see you. Do you want me to waken the servants and have a plaster put on this?" He gently touched the bump on my head as he spoke. It was the light coming from below that cast those haunting shadows on Kestrel's face, imbuing him with a charm not usually seen. Romantic was the word that came to mind.

"Is it bleeding?" I asked.

"No, it's swelling a little."

The effect of the romantic light and Kestrel's new attractiveness, his arm around my shoulder, and his fingers gently stroking my hair all conspired to make me as nervous as a deb. When nervous, I usually become curt. "If you'd stop pawing it, perhaps the swelling would go away," I suggested.

His reluctant smile widened to a derisive grin. "You have all the sentiment of a bandit, Marion Mathieson. Pawing indeed! You make me sound like a whelp—or a lecher. I can see you're back to your usual competent self, and I can get on with my job. I'll take you to your room first. Can you walk?" On this question, he finally removed his arm from my shoulder and his fingers from my hair, but a smile lingered in his eyes. A particularly bright, questioning smile.

"Wait!" In my eagerness to get back to work, I reached out and grabbed Kestrel's hand to prevent his leaving. A flicker of surprise shimmered over his features, lifting his eyebrows. His fingers closed over mine and squeezed. I felt a perfect fool, not knowing whether to return the pressure or wrench my hand away. The former seemed to forward, the latter too brusque, so I settled for doing nothing. I just let him hold my hand as though it were an empty glove. "We have to talk," I said.

"We'll talk later. Now I have to go after our quarry."

"I want to go with you. You haven't told me anything yet. Did you see who attacked me?"

"It was pitch black in the hallway."

"It must have been Sir Herbert. He was lurking in here, waiting to receive the letter from the spies."

"What were you doing here? And why have you changed your gown?"

— "I was outdoors taking a look around."

His face clenched like a fist, and his pale eyes sparkled angrily. "Outdoors! Dammit, Marion, this isn't some childish game. Those men are killers. You don't even have a pistol."

"That's one of the reasons I left my room. In fact, it's why I came in here, to look for one. Would you happen to know where Sir Herbert keeps them?"

"You won't require one. You'll be in your room, sleeping, and that's an order! But before you go—did you see anything outside?"

"There was no action going forth, so I peeked in windows instead. All I saw was Sir Herbert writing some letters, and you searching his study. Did you find anything?"

"No, I still think Sir Herbert's innocent."

"Innocent as an adder! Does this look as if he's innocent?" I demanded, pointing to my bump.

"He didn't do that. He's in his bedroom. I watched him go in."

"Well, you were obviously looking the other way when he came out again."

"No, he couldn't have got past me without being seen. Whoever attacked you didn't come downstairs in the past quarter of an hour. There was someone in here, waiting."

"Where did he go?"

"I didn't follow him. You were groaning. I thought you might be dying."

"You mean you let the spies escape while you came in here to force me to drink brandy? Oh, really, Kestrel! Castlereagh ought to be fired, hiring such an incompetent—" The murderous scowl on Kestrel's brow brought me to a stop.

"Next time I'll leave you to die. It's what you deserve. Didn't I tell you half a dozen times not to come here? Amateurs—a woman at that—cluttering up my work. I would have caught him if it weren't for you."

"Did you notice which way he went? Out the front door? Downstairs, where?"

"I don't know!" he shouted. "I lost him."

I just shook my head at this story. "He's been here, left the letters for Sir Herbert, and got away. It was Sir Herbert who knocked me out. Kestrel, we have to go after Longville. He means to turn that letter over to Boney. Either someone will come here for it, or he'll go somewhere to deliver it."

"It can't be Sir Herbert. He's not the type to betray his country. He's not short of cash. He has a prosperous farm here, and he loves every minute of it. What we're looking for is either someone desperate for money, someone with a grudge against England, or a love of France. Sir Herbert doesn't qualify on any score."

"If he loves it so much here, why did he go to Whitehall?"

"Because he's a patriot. He wanted to contribute to the fight against Boney."

"If not Sir Herbert, then it's someone in this household. This is where the spies were heading. You said there isn't another place nearby where anyone works at the Foreign Office. That's were the leak starts."

"I have a few other ideas," Kestrel mentioned casually, but my most avid questioning didn't add one iota to my knowledge.

"And now you must go to your room," he said. "I've wasted too much time." He rose and kicked aside one of my gloves, which I had removed while looking for the tinderbox. "What's this?" he asked, eyes alight. "A glove—a very small glove. It's a lady's!"

"It's mine."

He turned it over in his hands, noticing its sorry condition from climbing the ivy. "You must have used it to fight the pashas," he said, and tossed it to me.

'No, it was climbing out the window tonight that did the mischief."

Kestrel turned his head slowly and stared at me as though I were a tiger. "Do you mean to tell me you clambered out the upstairs window? You might have fallen and killed yourself."

"I might have, but I didn't. I was fine till Sir Herbert koshed me with something. I wonder what he used."

I got to my feet, and when the room stopped spinning, I looked around for the weapon. Lying near the door was a riding crop. Kestrel picked it up and we looked at it by the light of the one candle, now residing on the table. It was a dainty affair, slender, with ornamental brass rings embedded in the handle. You could tell to look at it that Sir Herbert wouldn't be caught dead in a ditch with such an elegant trifle.

"It must be Nel's," Kestrel said, frowning.

"Her father probably picked it up in the hall on his way in to kosh me," I said airily.

"Whoever was here didn't know you would come. He was here waiting for someone or something else."

"Perhaps Nel left it lying about. It's not important. These other ideas of yours, Kestrel—"

"My foremost idea is to lock you into your room. And nail the window shut," he added grimly.

With this little clue that he didn't mean to take me into his confidence, I wasted no more time in argument. I just held my head as though I could bearly stand the pain, and went upstairs, hoping to give the impression I was on my way to bed. Kestrel wore an extremely suspicious look as I walked past him. "Are you sure you're all right?" he asked.

"At the risk of boring you, Lord Kestrel, I have suffered worse torment in other lands and survived."

On this piece of noble hogwash, I left the room and darted upstairs to discuss developments with Ronald. Imagine my shock to find Miss Longville sitting on his chair, weeping buckets into his handkerchief. She was wearing a rather chic blue riding habit and chapeau cocked over one eye. From the condition of Ronald's handkerchief, a monogrammed one I had stitched with my own fingers, I estimated she had been watering it for longer than a few minutes.

I hardly knew what to say. "What on earth is the matter, Miss Longville?" I asked.

She put the wet linen to her nose and bawled louder. Ronald gave a grimace that indicated she might notice I had changed my gown. I didn't see much danger of Miss Longville having an attack of common sense when she was so distraught, nor did she. I went to sit by Ronald on the side of his bed.

"Nel was going to run away," he explained. "I heard footsteps and opened my door just as she was about to go downstairs. I convinced her to come in here and discuss the matter with me."

"She shouldn't be here alone with you."

"You're here!" he pointed out.

"I wasn't when she arrived."

Ronald batted it aside. "It's the most incredible thing you can imagine, Marion. Her papa is forcing her to marry Alfred Harcourt. She doesn't care for him in the least."

"The foolish man," I tsked. The name Bernard Kemp was in my mind, and I decided to test it. "But where did you think to go, Miss Longville? Do you have someone who would take you in?"

She lifted her tearstained eyes long enough to hiccough and nod an affirmative. "A relative?" I asked slyly. She shook her head no.

"It's another man," Ronald informed me. "A Mr. Kemp. Nel thinks she's in love with him."

"And are you quite certain Mr. Kemp loves you, Nel?" I asked gently. As Ronald was Nel'ing her, I decided to make free of her name as well. The unusual circumstances warranted it. It was all the style that night. Kestrel had called me Marion. I wondered what his Christian name was. The blue riding bonnet nodded vigorously.

"Mr. Kemp is well to do, is he?" I asked, shaking my head to Ronald to indicate it was not the case. The blue bonnet remained still, save for a little jiggle as she hiccoughed again into Ronald's linen. "I would want to make very sure he wasn't just marrying me for my money, before I threw my reputation to the wind by a runaway match," I added.

Two watery eyes were raised to Ronald in supplication. And he, the gudgeon, smiled his encouragement at her. "Nel assures me the attachment is long-standing," he explained.

"But is he attached to the money, or the lady?" I repeated. "Does Mr. Kemp have a fortune of his own? Or is he the sort of wastrel who ran through his fortune, and is now looking about for some guileless peahead to hand hers over to him?"

"He made some poor investments," Ronald said leniently.

"Is that French for saying he's a pauper?"

Nel managed to get her mouth open and answer for herself. "I have twenty-five thousand from Mama. It is my own money, and Papa can't stop me from having it when I am married."

"No, nitwit, but he can withhold his own fortune," I said frankly. "Longville Manor is worth five or ten times that. Do you mean to throw it all away for some devil-may-care lad who hasn't enough respect for you to settle down and earn his living, if he has no money?''

"Bernard isn't a pauper!" she said proudly. "He has a fine curricle and the best jackets in the county. He is learning the shipping business.''

"Then let him learn it, and earn a proper home to take you to before he marries you. Where did you and Bernard plan to live?''

She moved her shoulders uncomfortably. It was clear as glass she hadn't given the mere detail of a roof over her head any consideration whatsoever. "I must go," she said, and began gathering up reticule and gloves.

As she wore her riding habit, it occurred to me she might have been carrying a riding crop. But Ronald had encountered her at the top of the stairs, so she couldn't be my assailant. "Is Mr. Kemp waiting for you somewhere?" I asked. A crafty look settled on her plump, rather childish features.

She turned, ignoring me, to speak to Ronald. "Thank you, Mr. Kidd. I know you want to help me, but I must do this. I will not be forced into marrying Alfred Harcourt. I can't stand the man.''

"I wish you would reconsider, Nel," Ronald implored.

"I've thought and argued and begged Papa, but he says I must marry Alfred, before he changes his mind and has Miss Stokely. I have no choice. Surely you can see that.''

"Let me speak to your father, Nel," I said. "When he learns how desperate you are, I believe he'll reconsider.''

"Marion's very good at persuading people to do what they don't want to do," Ronald told her.

She cast an assessing look at me and took her decision. "Very well, I'll wait till tomorrow, but I won't marry Alfred Harcourt.''

"That's a wise decision," I said, and smiled in relief.

"Now go back to your bed, Miss Longville, and try not to worry. I promise you one thing: If your papa insists on your marrying Mr. Harcourt, you can come to stay with me in London till he changes his mind."

She looked her thanks—to Ronald! Really, the girl had no social graces. I didn't in the least relish having her around my neck, but on the other hand, I do not go along with parents forcing their children into unwanted matches. I would always be ready to take a stand on that matter. "Would you like Ronald to go and tell Mr. Kemp what happened? Is he waiting somewhere nearby for you?" I asked.

"Oh no. I was going to go to his house," the idiot replied. I began to think I had done Mr. Kemp a favor as well in ridding him of this peagoose.

Ronald took her to the door and watched while she slipped into her room. "That was very kind of you, Marion, offering Nel a refuge," he said.

"I hope to God it doesn't come to that, but if it does, I won't renege on the offer. I don't suppose you've had much opportunity to keep watch on the window?"

"No, but nothing happened while I was watching. I say, Marion, is that a lump on your forehead? What happened—did you fall off the vine?"

"No, Sir Herbert knocked me out," I said, and recounted my adventure. "Get dressed at once, Ronald. I hope we haven't lost track of Kestrel. He's convinced that scoundrel of a Sir Herbert is innocent, just because they're in the sheep-raising business together. I'm convinced it was Longville who knocked me out. Who else could it be?"

"Of course it was. A man who'd force his daughter into a bad marriage obviously has no scruples. But never mind Kestrel, it's Sir Herbert we must watch."

"Kestrel said he had some other ideas as well. Longville might have some of his servants in on it with him. I daresay that's what he meant. While you dress, I'll creep along the hall and see if I catch Herbert leaving his room. Not that I think for one minute he is *in* it.''

I didn't know which room was Sir Herbert's, but it would be one of those with a closed door. Nel's was closed, my own, and a few others along the hallway. I tiptoed past them, and from one I heard the unmistakable sounds of a man snoring. Ronald and Kestrel were the only other two gentlemen in the house, and I knew neither of them were sawing logs. I felt a sinking sensation that Sir Herbert had already completed his night's dirty work while I was otherwise occupied. Such was his villainy that he could place his head on a pillow and sleep like an honest man, after betraying his country to Napoleon, and his daughter to Alfred Harcourt. Hanging was too good for him.

When Ronald came out, I told him about the snoring. He was more interested in Nel. He looked lovingly at her closed doorway. There were no snores from that direction. ''I hope she meant it when she said she'd wait till morning,'' he worried.

''What on earth do you see in that child?'' I asked, for it was clear as a pikestaff Ronald had a tendre for her.

''Why, she's so pretty!'' he answered.

''A provincial squab, pretty? A watering pot with neither sense nor judgement nor pride, to be running to a man in the middle of the night, begging him to run away with her? You've lost the use of your wits, Mr. Kidd.''

''But she's so helpless, Marion. Not like you, able to handle anything. A man feels the urge to help a lady like that.''

I remembered Kestrel's kindness to me downstairs when I had been attacked. A lady in distress had momentarily softened the heart of even that wretched man. If a lady had any taste for marriage, she would be wise to feign incompetence, or hire some cruel stepfather to force her into an unwanted marriage.

"Do you happen to know Kestrel's Christian name?" I asked.

"I've no idea. Why do you want to know that?"

"Just curious."

Chapter Eight

We slipped quietly downstairs into the dark hallway. Ronald wanted to see where I'd been attacked. I took him to the room, we closed the door, lit a candle, and looked around for clues. "Obviously this is where Sir Herbert received the message from the spy," I explained. "The door leading outside was left off the latch. I believe the letter had already been passed over to him, and he delivered it to whomever he reports to after knocking me out, then went up to bed."

"Then you're saying the whole thing is a fait accompli," Ronald pointed out. "You didn't see the man with the letter enter by the French doors, or come out again while you were lurking there?"

"No, not while I was watching."

"Why would Sir Herbert have hung about in the dark room after he got what he was after? It would be more logical for him to turn it over to his contact at once." Ronald has a way of using jargon that would make you think he'd been an expert forever at whatever new matter we're involved in. That "contact," which Kestrel had used only once, came out as smooth as cream.

"The other possibility is that he hadn't received it yet," I pointed out. "He thought I was the spy, and when he realized I wasn't, he knocked me out."

"And went upstairs to sleep without receiving the

letter?'' Ronald asked, with a face that said he expected better of me.

"If he wasn't waiting for the letter, then why was he here?"

"There's no proof he was here. You don't know it was Sir Herbert."

"As Kestrel explained, the leak begins at the F.O.," I said, and peered to see if Ronald recognized the initials. He nodded his comprehension. "There are no other F.O. employees living near here. This is where the spies were bringing the letter, according to Kestrel."

Ronald lifted a doubtful brow. "I thought Kestrel believed Sir Herbert innocent."

"He doesn't like to admit otherwise, but he acknowledges there's no one else it could be. At least that's what he said."

"Yes, what Kestrel *said*. And according to you, Kestrel only came to your assistance after you'd been knocked senseless. Who's to say he isn't the one who hit you? What I'm getting at is that Kestrel lives nearby, and *he* works at the F.O. We only know what he chooses to tell us, Marion, and at times it sounded like a bag of moonshine. We both noticed he didn't put up any fight when he was robbed. It almost seemed he wanted to give over that letter."

"He explained all that. He did want to give it over, so he could follow the spies and find the ringleader. If you're implying that he is the leak, Ronald, you're sadly off the mark. Why would he bother chasing after those spies if all he wanted was to give secrets to Boney?"

"Perhaps because you questioned him about his peculiar behavior—the way he left his pistol in the curricle, and drove the coach instead of being ready to defend himself. He needed some explanation when you chided him, and that's when he came up with the story of trying to catch the ringleader. I found that tale of the cut

102

wheel pin in London pretty fishy myself. I believe he had it done so he could transfer to the coach. The timing of it was very convenient.''

"Why would he want to transfer to the coach?"

"So he'd have witnesses that he was robbed, and didn't just hand over the orders. That way they'll believe him innocent in London, and give him other documents to deliver. When you insisted on helping him— do you remember how he fought it?"

"The only reason we're here is because he thought I had money," I nodded.

"He had to go through with the farce of letting on he was following spies because we stuck to him like burrs all day. We never caught a sight of any spies.''

"No, but we found Cooke's Bible, and the merchant's trinkets. And the farmer who let us jump his fence saw them. He said there *were* three men headed this way.''

"We know there were three men," Ronald persisted. "Naturally they were coming this way—toward the coast at least. I expect they went to Dover or Romney Marsh, where the smugglers are as thick as crickets, and Kestrel's led us off here on a merry chase while the documents go off scot-free to Boney. He was just distracting us, Marion. If you weren't so busy rolling your eyes at him, you'd have seen it long ago.''

"Let us not get into a dissertation on rolling eyes, Mr. Kidd. I never saw such a disgusting display in my life as your smiling and simpering at that half wit of a girl. If I hadn't chanced along, you would personally have escorted her into the hands of Mr. Kemp, to fritter away her fortune. I was not rolling my eyes at Kestrel— though now that you mention it, he was trying to flirt with me when I was lying on the sofa.''

"Was he, by Jove?"

"Yes, and that's why he did it! He didn't want me to start thinking of other things, such as his unexplained presence in the room. Though really, I did hear a scuffle

103

in the hall." I really had seen a shadow of concern in his eyes, too, as he leaned over me.

"You were half-senseless. You could have imagined it."

"If the spies are home free with the documents, why does Kestrel bother hanging around here?" I pondered this a moment and found my own explanation. "Unless having told us there were spies on the way, he must act as though it were true. I mentioned going to Castlereagh to offer our services, you know, and Kestrel wouldn't want us telling any tales that jeopardized his reputation. He was quick to discourage me. He's trying to convince us that his story was true. We're wasting our time, Ronald. That letter is already on its way to France. I'm going to bed."

Just when I thought everything was settled, Ronald came up with a new idea. "Of course, it's just possible that Kestrel was supposed to meet the spies here tonight, and plan new strategies," he said. 'I mean, a man like Kestrel—he isn't just some minor cog in the machinery. He's obviously the ringleader himself. As he's remaining here, at Longville Manor, there must be some reason."

"The reason is that he's trying to convince us he was telling the truth."

"Perhaps," Ronald said doubtfully. "Or perhaps he's arranging how the next set of orders from the F.O. can be stolen. He won't want to go on using highwaymen forever. That would begin to look suspicious after a while. You run along up to bed if you're tired, Marion. I believe I'll just hang around down here for a while and see what happens."

He knew there wasn't a chance in a million I would retire when he said that. I disliked the notion of Kestrel being guilty of treason, but that was mere sentiment. Just because a man has long eyelashes and a gentle touch on your hair is no reason to be blind to reality.

All men's chests are warm and protective at close range, even traitors'. Ronald could be right. The very fact that it was Ronald and not myself who saw the possibility showed me I had not been sticking to facts as closely as I should, and usually did. I, who prided myself on using my head! On one thing I was in complete agreement with my secretary. If Kestrel was guiltily involved at all, he was no one's pawn. He would be the ringleader. Why he should have involved himself on the wrong side wasn't clear, but there is no accounting for treachery. He may have imagined he suffered some wrong at he hands of the government, or he may be doing it for money.

As we stood, thinking, there was a little movement of the doorknob. We exchanged a frightened look, I blew out the candle and flew behind the sofa, and Ronald just stood like a moonling while the door opened and someone came in. I don't know how he knew who was there, but Kestrel said, "Is that you, Mr. Kidd?"

"Kestrel?"

"Yes, what are you doing here?"

"I was just—Marion told me about being attacked, and I came down to see if I could find any clues."

There was the scraping of a flint, and from behind the sofa I discerned a slight lessening of the shadows.

"Did you find anything?" Kestrel asked. He sounded worried. The criminal does return to the scene of the crime, I've read.

"No, I was just beginning to look. I daresay it was the spies who hit her," Ronald said leadingly. "What do you think, Kestrel?"

"I expect she walked into a door and was ashamed to say so." My fingers curled into fists, and I had to force myself not to point out that I was nowhere near a door when I was hit. "Does she always go off halfcocked as she did on this occasion?"

Ronald cleared his throat nervously, very much aware

of my listening ears, and said, "She's rather head-strong."

"The woman is a menace to society. I don't know how you put up with her. Is there any truth at all to those tall tales she rattles off with such nonchalance?"

"Every word is true—nearly." I was smiling to myself till Ronald added that demeaning "nearly." "She omits *my* part in our experiences. Actually, *I* am the one who went out to argue with Prince Nasar in the desert. Marion did back me up very efficiently, however."

"If a quarter of what she's broadcasting so loudly to the world is true, there isn't a polite saloon in London that will be open to her." Hah! Tom Moore would be surprised to hear that! "Folks may go to hear her stories, but if she has in mind making a match, she's going about it the wrong way."

"Marion isn't interested in marriage."

"All women are interested in marriage," Kestrel said comprehensively. "Especially when they reach her years. How old is Miss Mathieson? Not much short of thirty, I should think?"

I tried to direct the thought into Ronald's head that he should shave half a decade from my thirty-two years, but the message didn't reach him.

"She's well over thirty," I heard my secretary say. Two years is hardly "well over"! "But she was never interested in marriage, even when she was the right age for it." Oh, thank you, Ronald. That was a brilliant speech. "In fact, she first went traveling to avoid her relatives' urgings that she settle down." Well, at least he got that right!

"Anyone special they had in mind for her?"

I knew I shouldn't have railed so hard against poor Mr. Lambert. "Some fish merchant," Ronald replied. Kestrel emitted a snort of amusement. Mr. Lambert was *not* a fish merchant. He was a very prosperous owner of a fishing fleet. The objection was not to his calling but his personal appearance, which too closely resembled the cod his ships brought home from the coast of Newfoundland.

"I should think those travels cost a pretty penny. Where did she get the blunt?" Kestrel enquired. What I longed to shout from behind the sofa was, where did Kestrel get the gall, inquiring so minutely into my background? I wished Ronald would give him a good set-down.

"Her family has money," Ronald said vaguely.

"Where does the family live?"

"They don't live anywhere." He made me sound like a gypsy! "Her parents are dead now. Her papa was a captain in the army. She followed the drum with him, which is where she got a taste for travel."

"I wonder Beau Douro didn't clean up the Peninsula long ago with Miss Mathieson to assist him."

Ronald laughed weakly, not knowing what answer would please me, but he knew he had overstepped the boundary in claiming he had confronted Nasar alone, while I "backed him up." We faced Nasar together, and it is my slight oversight in not including his name in that section of the memoirs that he was repaying me for. If he was a step ahead of me, it was no more than that.

Kestrel soon tired of discussing me. "Let's have a look around here for clues," he said, and lifted the candle to begin scouring the room to see what he'd left behind.

I hunched low behind the sofa, ready to move aside if he came that way. Ronald foresaw this possibility and lit a candle himself, ostentatiously looking behind the sofa and saying, "There's nothing here. Have you found anything, Lord Kestrel?"

"Nothing new. Just Miss Longville's riding crop, which was here earlier."

"That's odd!" I could hear the interest in Ronald's tone, and hoped the ninny wasn't about to blurt out Nel's little spree. He had too much respect for the girl to do so. "Anything else?" he asked.

"No, there's nothing here. I'm going down to the coast."

"What for?" Ronald asked suspiciously. It immediately occurred to me that this was the first time Kestrel had ever volunteered a single word of his activities. Why was he suddenly taking Ronald into his confidence?

"We still haven't intercepted the spies," Kestrel pointed out. "I thought they'd bring the letter here, but there's been more than enough time for it, and it hasn't turned up."

"Maybe Sir Herbert has got it already."

"No, he hasn't had any privacy. He was just in his office for a while, and I kept a watch on the door all the time. Sir Herbert can't be our man. But the spies were approaching Longville Manor. Someone here has already intercepted the letter. We must get it before it leaves the country. To reach France from here, it must go by sea. And that is why we're going down to the coast."

"I" had suddenly become "we," and as I crouched behind the sofa, I was struck with the awful idea that the only reason Kestrel wanted to get Ronald out of the house was to do away with him. My attachment to Ronald was of long standing. For a few years we had been together constantly, living through incredible dangers and excitements. He was as dear to me as a brother, and I couldn't let him fall into such danger. Yet to rise up from my concealment and suddenly announce my presence seemed equally impossible. Would it not be better to let Kestrel think he had Ronald alone, and follow them, providing protection from behind?

Ronald cleared his throat. "Er, does that mean you

108

want me to go with you, Kestrel?'' There was much less suspicion than eagerness in his voice.

''I could use some assistance. I would have taken you into my confidence earlier, Ronald, but I feared that would mean having Miss Mathieson hanging around our necks as well. This is no business for a lady. I must warn you, there's some danger in it. I confirmed from Sir Herbert earlier this evening that the smuggled shipment of brandy is expected tonight. I'm fairly certain the letter will go to France on that boat when it leaves. My hope is that we'll catch our contact from Longville Manor when the letter is delivered to the boat, as we obviously missed it earlier. We may have to deal with a cutthroat band of smugglers, which is why I could use your help. And obviously why I don't want Miss Mathieson involved.''

Mr. Kidd was addressed as Ronald to confer a spurious air of camaraderie. Whether it was that or the lure of danger, or the opportunity to pitch himself into an adventure denied me that convinced Ronald, I could not say. His reply, however, was ''I should be honored to assist you, Kestrel.'' He was too poor a liar to be pretending to believe Kestrel. He did believe him. I, being ''well over thirty,'' had to be wise for us both, and maintain my doubts, and my vigilance over Ronald. Though I wasn't too old to hope Kestrel was not a traitor. Beneath his impertinent question, there was a tone of interest about Miss Mathieson.

In my mind, I pictured the short ensuing silence was due to one of Kestrel's conning smiles. ''I wish you will call me Nick, as I've taken the liberty of using your Christian name.''

''That's odd!'' Ronald exclaimed, and laughed. Oh no! The idiot wasn't going to blurt out that I had asked if he knew Kestrel's name.

''It's short for Nicholas; not Old Nick—Satan.'' I breathed a small sigh of relief. It was short-lived.

"No, what is odd, Marion was just asking me a moment—a short while ago, when I spoke to her upstairs, what your name was."

"Was she indeed? You can tell her when next you two meet, not that she'll ever use it. You'll need some peace offering after beating her to the gun in catching the spies. But more importantly, you'll need some protection for tonight's escapade. Let's go to the armaments room now and find you something."

"Yes, by Jove, and this time I'll make sure the trigger ain't welded shut. Odd Marion didn't notice that." They both gave a superior little laugh at my oversight. You would think Ronald had been outside the door during the transaction, and not holding the pistol and praising its balance.

They left, taking the candles with them, and I stood up, to ease the cramps out of my knees. My humor was about as black as the room. I would crown Ronald with a water jug after this was over. A private secretary is not expected to announce his employer's most intimate secrets to the public. If he insists on doing so, he might at least get the facts straight. "Well over thirty"! Nick would think I was an antique. And like a typical man, Ronald hadn't even the wits to discover Kestrel's age, or anything about him.

All this would provide much rancorous repining later, and much angry debate, but for the moment, I had more important things to do. Paramount amongst them was to discover the location of the armaments room, and avail myself of a weapon. Ronald might at least have had the wits to leave the door open. He knew I would be following. The damn knob began to squawk when I turned it. I had to wait till the men were beyond hearing to open it and follow them. It was almost impossible to see anything in the hallway. It was only the telltale glow of the candle ahead that showed me the location of the armaments room, a few doors down and to the right.

Naturally, I had to wait till Ronald had procured a weapon and left before I was after mine.

One cannot choose a weapon in the dark, which meant wasting precious minutes finding the tinderbox and a lamp. A paneled room sprang into dim view, its walls plastered with all manner of weapons, mostly ancient. There were crossed halberds aplenty from the fifteenth century. A handle six feet long was longer than I required, nor did I particularly wish to spear the enemy. There were pikes and battle-axes, some handles with spiked heads attacked, and standing guard below it all a row of rusty suits of armor and shields. I was surprised a sheepbreeder housed such an arsenal, but what was not there was a modern pistol. I could see the spot on the wall where one had been removed for Ronald. The open ammunition box for it still sat on the table.

What guns remained on the wall were antique weapons and hunting guns, great, cumbersome things fit for shooting elephants. I had never used one, and hadn't a single notion even what sort of ammunition would be required. Precious moments were slipping away. If I waited longer, I'd lose track of the men entirely. Desperate, I removed the shortest sword I could find on the wall—really, more like a long dagger—and with that under my jacket, I blew out the candle and left.

Kestrel and Ronald had left the house by then. At least I knew their destination. The coast lay to the south. I hurried to the front door and nearly capsized Miss Longville, on her way out. The sly thing only pretended to agree to my offer of speaking to her papa. She was no more pleased to see me than I was to meet her.

"What are you doing here?" she demanded angrily.

"You're supposed to be in bed!" I replied, in the same tone.

"You're not my mama. I can go out if I want to."

I took a firm grip on her elbow, ruing every second's delay. "We shall see what your papa has to say about this." I prayed she was susceptible to a threat, for my feeling was that her papa was not in the house at all, but en route to the coast. Fortunately for me, she was.

"Oh, Miss Mathieson!" she sniffled, and pulled out a dainty lace-edged handkerchief. "I must go. Bernard is waiting for me."

"You said he was not!"

"I didn't want you to know. I must see him."

"For God's sake, go to bed, Nel. This is no time for tears and tantrums."

"But I must. I only wanted to see him. I have written everything we agreed on in a letter, and only meant to give it to him and leave."

Desperate to be rid of her, I said, "Give me the letter. I'll deliver it for you, with your apologies. Where were you to meet him?"

"Our trysting place is the big willow tree, down at the end of our private road—just where it turns off from the main road. He'll be waiting there. Bernard doesn't like me to have to go off Papa's property, yet we cannot meet too near the house, in case of being seen."

A model of consideration, this Bernard. "Give me the letter," I said impatiently.

She handed me a letter, romantically bound up in a satin handkerchief folder, tied with ribbons and scented with violet. "Tell him—tell him I still love him," she said, dabbing at her tears.

"Of course. Now you go back to bed, Nel. I'll report to you in the morning what Bernard said."

She nodded and went back upstairs. Her pace was slow, her shoulders sagging. There was an air of resignation about her that had been absent earlier. I felt she would really stick to our bargain this time. At long last I was free to continue on my way. I turned the knob and walked out into the cool night.

Chapter Nine

The sky overhead bore a resemblance to last night's sullen gray canopy. The wind was up tonight, too, but it had not that oppressive feeling of imminent rain. There was moisture in the air, carried on the breeze from the ocean, tanged with salt and the aroma of seaweed. It moved the branches overhead, and pulled at my skirt. This was a night when my trousers would have been welcome. It was rough walking in dainty slippers over the cinder road down to the beach. Was it only last night I had slogged through the torrents, finally finding sanctuary in an abandoned cottage? It seemed an age ago. England was proving less dull than I feared. Aurelia was presently involved in the treachery of her own family, but when next she appeared between covers, she might find herself mixed up with spies and smugglers.

Meanwhile it was I who was involved, and I must keep my wits about me. As I hastened southward, I peered around the tall and sedate poplars and the more frivolous spreading lime trees that bordered Longville's drive. Something moved in the road just in front of me, and I nearly screamed, till I learned it was just a small night creature. In my fright, I dropped Nel's letter. Another nuisance. I wouldn't deliver it till after the more important business was settled, unless Kemp was actually there waiting at the willow tree, in which case I'd hand it to him and be on my way.

When matters of national importance are at stake, one's first concern should be the safety of the country, but as I went skimming through the night, it was of Ronald's safety that I thought. And possibly Kestrel's, if he was indeed innocent. That question bothered me considerably. How would I know? Of course, if I found Ronald backed up against a tree with Kestrel's muzzle against his chest, there would be no question. If, on the other hand, they were together, Ronald not in immediate jeopardy, what course should I take? I would conceal myself nearby and watch. Childish dreams whirled in my head of a smuggler creeping up on Kestrel, myself behind the smuggler, knocking him cold and saving Kestrel's life. Then he would eat his words about this not being a place for a lady.

Before I reached the end of the private drive, the public road was visible ahead, a white ribbon in the night, going to Dover and Hythe. As I hastened toward it, I saw on my left a sprawling willow tree drooping its ropes to the ground. I took a close look, but there was no sign of Mr. Kemp. If he had been waiting since Nel first tried to go to him, he would have given up and gone home. That was an hour ago. I wouldn't bother stopping at all. I glanced to the left, prepared to go by.

Even knowing he might be there, Kemp's sudden appearance scared the wits out of me. He didn't make a sound, but just detached himself from the shadows and swooped down on me like a bird of prey. Before I knew what was afoot, he had me in his arms, his lips burning a hot kiss on mine, while his strong arms crushed me against him. Expecting Nel, he had mistaken me for her. It flashed into my head that this was a very passionate man for little Miss Longville to have attached. He kissed like a well-seasoned veteran in the war of love. Could this be Bernard Kemp, or was it— The face

114

in my mind as those bold lips seared mine was Kestrel's. It was Kestrel's arms that bound me to him with such ardor. I felt an unexpected, quivering response to his passion. It started at the base of my skull and trembled down my spine, making my arms weak, and my breath short.

After a lusty embrace, he held me off at arm's length, and I saw that, contrary to my wild imaginings, it was not Kestrel I faced, but a total stranger. A dark, dashing, handsome man with teeth that flashed in the shadows as he smiled. "Darling!" Then he stopped. A quick frown replaced the smile of welcome. "Who the hell are you?" he demanded roughly.

I detached myself with what dignity I could. "Mr. Kemp, I assume?"

"Who are you?" he repeated.

"I am Miss Longville's emissary. She was unable to get away tonight, and asked me to deliver her apologies, and this letter." On this speech, I produced the satin folder. Kemp, for I assumed he must be, reached out and snatched it eagerly.

In a great rush to be off, I turned to leave. "Oh, and she said to tell you she loves you."

He was still holding me by one arm. I looked at his hand rather peremptorily. "I am in a hurry, Mr. Kemp."

"But who are you?" he repeated.

"If you must know, I am Miss Mathieson, a house guest of the Longvilles'."

"I didn't hear they had company."

"Well, they have. And now, if you'll kindly release me."

He dropped my arm, and I proceeded on my way. He wasn't a step behind me. "Where are you going? The Manor is back that way," he said, pointing back up the drive. There was a certain something in his tone that made me walk more quickly.

115

"I am not blind, Mr. Kemp. I know where the house is. I am not going to the house."

He soon overtook me. His fingers seized my arm again in a ruthless grasp. "What are you up to?" he scowled.

"I am on a very important private mission. Let go of me at once or—"

He pulled me roughly off the drive, into the shadows of the trees. My first spasm of alarm shot a little higher. "Not so fast, miss. I'll have an explanation, if you please."

Much as I disliked to humor the man, he was stronger than I, and extremely persistent. Telling him what he wanted to know seemed the fastest way to be free of him. The urgency of my mission would surely gain my freedom. "If you must know, I am on my way to catch some spies, and it is an extremely urgent matter."

"What spies? There are no spies around here."

"You are mistaken. There are, and my friend is in some danger of being killed by them."

"Who's your friend? Kestrel?" His voice was cold, ruthless, and held a fair share of contempt.

Claiming friendship with Kestrel seemed a poor idea. "His name is Mr. Kidd. He's my secretary."

"What's a lady doing with a secretary?"

Experience has taught me to keep a calm voice when my insides are shaking. Yes, I admit I was shaking. Though I have been through much, danger still unsettles me. Our officers in the Peninsula have a saying, Bravery does not consist in feeling no fear, but in overcoming fear. "I employ him to conduct my business correspondence and other matters of a private nature," I answered with seeming composure. Mr. Kemp appeared much less handsome than before. There was a hard look on his face, and a rough, indeed menacing, edge to his voice.

"Tell me more about this spy business," he said. As

he still gripped my arm firmly, I was less curt than I wished to be.

I quickly outlined the situation. His eyes narrowed and he listened closely. "So you think there's a letter going out to France on the smuggling boat tonight?"

"Yes, if we can't prevent it."

"Who, exactly, is we?"

"Mr. Kidd and myself."

"I saw Kestrel in town today. Is he here, too?"

"He might be joining us," I said vaguely, but it didn't fool Kemp.

"Where are Kestrel and Kidd?"

"They went down to the coast. I don't know exactly where, but Kestrel seemed to know the spot. Perhaps you would know where the smugglers land?" I asked.

"Are they armed?"

"I assume smugglers and spies arm themselves."

"I mean Kestrel!" His voice was quite impatient.

"Of course they are."

"How long ago did they head out?"

"Good gracious, so many things have happened. It must be a quarter of an hour to twenty minutes. Now please, let me go."

I saw the look of indecision on his face. I thought that, like Ronald, Mr. Kemp had a mind to pitch himself into the fray. He was a strong man, with presumably a good knowledge of the coast. Perhaps he'd help me. Imagine my astonishment when he drew a pistol out from beneath his cape and leveled it at me. An ugly laugh rent the air. "You're as stupid as Nel," he said.

I was certain he was going to shoot me. I still think it was only his fear of the resulting noise that deterred him. In any case, I knew I was in mortal danger, and my instinctive response was to open my mouth and holler. Kemp's reaction was so swift, I didn't get out more than a grunt before he clamped a hand over my lips and dragged me under the willow tree, with the leaves and branches scratching at my face. The branches touched the ground all around. Under the tree, it was like a private room, pitch black and airless and very still.

"One squawk out of you and I'll kill you," he growled. There was an air about the man that left no doubt as to his seriousness. He pushed me down on the ground and stuck a leather glove into my mouth. Within seconds I was trussed up like a goose for the oven, bound wing and leg—wing with his spotted Belcher kerchief, and once my hands were useless, he ripped a piece from my skirt and tied my ankles together. Did it all in the darkness, without a single word, which was somehow more threatening than abuse or curses.

Truth to tell, I was so relieved he didn't kill me that I didn't object to being tied and gagged. The better part of valor is still discretion. When Kemp had me helpless on the ground, he ripped off another strip of my skirt and bound me to the trunk of the willow tree. This done, he peered through the willow branches and soon disappeared through them. With his departure, some tiny shred of peace returned, enough at least to try to figure out why he had done this senseless thing.

I had done him a favor, bringing him Nel's letter. Why then had he treated me like an enemy? And Nel— 'You're as stupid as Nel!' he had scoffed. Yet that passionate kiss when he thought I was she. What hypocrites men are, and what fools we women. Kemp was playing a double game, and before too long, glimmerings of it began to dawn on me. Had I not been so startled and frightened by Kemp, no doubt the light would have dawned sooner. Meanwhile I was making strenuous efforts to free myself. I had spat out the glove as soon as he left, but shouting was not recommended, lest it bring him back. Freeing my hands, tied behind my back, was the first item of priority. He had bound them so tightly the blood couldn't circulate properly. Already my fingers were becoming numb.

Considered in the relative peace and quiet of the willow's branches, Kemp's close questioning about where I was going and what I was doing appeared ominous. He showed too much interest in my story of spies and smugglers. And I had told him too much—exactly where Kestrel and Ronald were going, that they were armed, what they meant to do. None of it seemed to surprise him either. He had spoken of Kestrel in a disdainful way. As a local fellow, he'd know Kestrel by reputation at least. In short, I feared that what I had done was to send either a spy or a smuggler or both after Ronald and Kestrel. There was no doubt that Kemp was up to some chicanery. His eagerness to go haring off to the coast confirmed it if his questions did not.

The next point to determine was whether he was only a smuggler, or whether he was a spy as well, which was much more serious. He had been lurking at the willow tree for over an hour. Had he met with our three spies while there, and got the letter from them? Was that why Sir Herbert had behaved so innocently, because he was innocent? But who had hit me then in the darkness at Longville? Kestrel was less suspect now, since Kemp disparaged him.

And Kestrel said it wasn't Sir Herbert. I remembered Nel's riding crop. And Nel in her riding habit, sneaking off to meet Bernard Kemp. Ronald said he had intercepted her at the head of the stairs, but it was possible she had been running up, not down. Was it Nel who had koshed me? And what was she doing in that room, late at night, in her riding habit? Oh, planning to go to Bernard, of course, but she'd gone to the front door the second time, not out the French doors of the library.

My fingers were completely numb, making it difficult to free them. They felt like sausages, that fat with blood, and that useless. I concluded that my attacker was Nel, and with my mind centered on her, the next conclusion was obvious. Nel was the one who had received the letter from the spies. She had behaved rather strangely when we first came to Longville Manor, as I considered it. She had arrived with suspicious promptitude at the little parlor where the butler had sequestered us—almost as though she had been waiting for someone to come. Then she had dismissed the butler, and turned that brightly questioning look on Ronald. She had asked what had been done with our "personal things"—had gone herself to see them, and looked surprised that we had no luggage. No letter; that was what surprised her. She had thought either Ronald or I to be her contact.

Oh, she had been careful, in case she was mistaken, but she had mentioned she and I could be "alone" in her room. I thought at the time it was a strange thing to say. When I didn't produce the letter, she went hopping off to Ronald, hoping he might have it. I remembered seeing her come from his room after I changed. The ninny was working with Bernard Kemp to smuggle secrets to Boney. She went to London with her papa, and must rifle his secret correspondence there. And when she couldn't rifle, she discovered from her papa when orders were on the way to the army, and informed Bernard, who set out spies to steal them.

Who would have thought it of that witless creature? Even Bernard called her stupid. He was only using her, of course. But she couldn't be totally unaware of what she was doing. The pains she had gone to that night to smuggle his letter to him . . . Oh lord! She had smuggled the letter through me! That was what was wrapped up in that satin handkerchief case. And I, like a gossoon, delivered it straight into his hands. I might very well be charged for conspiracy if it were ever found out.

In my agitation I gave a harder yank at my hands and got one free. The other soon pulled loose as well. My fingers ached like the very devil. They were hot and stinging, with a million needles prickling them. After massaging them a minute, I could grasp my little dagger and cut my feet free, and eventually my body from the willow trunk. When circulation had returned to all my limbs and I was able to stand, I peered through the willow branches. All was quiet beyond. I parted the branches and slipped out into fresh air.

On the far side of the public road, there was an escarpment leading down to the beach. Below, the ocean spread off into the distance, a glittering, wimpled sheet of silver, ruffled to whitecaps by the wind. Though the moon was invisible, some beams penetrated the cloud blanket, conferring a metallic sheen to the surface. Where I stood, the descent was impossible by foot. Rock cliffs fell sheer to the sea. The same condition prevailed to my right. I glanced to the left, and saw this was the way I must go. There the rock cliff was broken into huge boulders, juts of smooth rock but with smaller ones between, allowing a foothold to the shingled beach below. Between the darkness and the distance, it was impossible to tell whether there was any human life lurking there, but I could see clearly enough there were no smuggling boats nor any other vessels on the ocean. With the moon casting that eerie light, the ocean reminded me of the Bedouin desert at night. The sand will gleam like that when the moon is full, and if there has been a wind that day, the surface is rippled into solid waves. Something of the same feeling of vast emptiness, a haunting intimation of eternity. It was awe-inspiring, almost a holy feeling. I personally never felt anywhere near so close to God in church. I sent a silent prayer heavenward.

Shaking away this vague sense of desolation, I examined the left cliff more closely, choosing my route and hoping for a sight of Ronald or Kestrel. Or less happily, of Bernard Kemp sneaking up behind them.

Reluctantly, my fingers closed over the dagger. I wouldn't be caught off guard again. My position atop the cliff in open terrain was not a safe one. I ducked my head down and scampered along till I reached a spot where descent seemed possible, though far from easy. The size of those boulders was deceptive from the distance. At closer range, they proved to be huge—some of them the length of my body, and the same width. If I lost my footing, not unlikely in the slippery-bottomed red slippers I still wore, I would plunge down the rock scree to my death. This was not the time to lose courage. I sat on the edge of the cliff, turned my body around by putting my weight on my hands, and hoisted myself off the edge, facing the cliff. I got a toehold and began the descent. It occurred to me that if I had chosen the wrong spot to go down, I would have the devil's own time ever getting back up again.

After I had descended more than fifty feet, there seemed a distinct possibility that I would be plastered to the rock wall for the rest of my life—which wouldn't be very long either. I had got myself into an impossible position, clinging for my life to a sheer wall of cliff, with no foothold available below, and not much possibility of being able to hoist myself back up to the top to start over again at some other spot. In short, I was stranded. I hardly dared turn my head, lest that bit of motion should dislodge my cramped fingers. After staring at the wall for a minute, with beads of perspiration popping out on my forehead and all along my spine, I finally did carefully turn my head to the right. Ranging about three yards distant in that direction, the descent appeared easier. The large boulders had crumbled to smaller rocks. If I could work my way sideways, I thought I could make it down to the beach without undue threat to life or limb.

I slid one foot to the right, and felt a nice strong bulge. It took my weight without giving way. I jiggled my right foot over on the bulge to make room for the left. I was proceeding nicely to the safer passage at the right. Another ledge of stone met my searching foot. I moved again. Before long, I found myself safely ensconced amidst the smaller rocks, ready to scamper down.

From the safety of my new perch, I turned to scan the ocean. A ship had come into view. It was a low, dark lump in the water—what they call a lugger, I believe. It had three masts, and square sails hanging obliquely. It bore no lights but advanced secretively in the dark, as a smuggling boat would do. I watched a moment to gauge its direction. It was ploughing straight for shore, toward a little inlet about fifty yards along the beach. My heart was hammering like a drum in my chest. The critical moment approached, and I was alone, with only a dagger to face a whole smuggling band of spies. Where were Ronald and Kestrel? Had Kemp overtaken them? Did they lie somewhere on the rocks, with their throats slit? This line of thought was mere weakness. I reminded myself that the better part of valor was discretion, and remained discreetly motionless, looking all around.

The lugger had lowered her sails and stopped several yards from the beach. As heads appeared on deck, the beach was suddenly peopled with a dozen or more men. They popped out as if by magic from cracks and crevices where they had been waiting. The men on board hoisted barrels into the water, and those on the beach waded out to recover them. The breeze carried a low murmur of muted voices, indistinguishable, but they were happy, carefree voices, not the murderous accents of killers.

Was this nothing more than a band of the Gentlemen at work? I fervently prayed it was so. As I watched from my perch, I saw three of the men on the lugger clamber overboard, wade to the beach, and walk off apart from the others. I watched, horrified, as they approached the beach immediately below me. Then they began to climb up the cliff.

Chapter Ten

For about sixty seconds I just clung to my rock. My instinctive response at the smugglers' approach was to hide. It seemed an easy enough thing to do, surrounded by loose rocks and stones as I was. The incline at this lower level was not precariously steep, nor was it very likely they would see me, as their attention was concentrated on the chore of climbing. Once I was cowering safely behind a large rock, however, I realized I had behaved like the veriest poltroon. Was I not to lift a finger to stop them, after having come this far? Was this the behavior of a woman who had almost single-handedly quelled an Arab revolt—and worse, bragged of it to Kestrel? I must tackle this new enemy, let the harvest be what it might. While this fit of heroics was upon me, I eased my head out from behind my rock and peeped down at the men climbing up.

What I saw reminded me, in retrospect, of a French farce, though at the time it was far too dangerous a sight to conjure up so frivolous an image. Spread out below me, and seen at an angle as though I were looking down a long staircase to the ground, was a series of people in hiding along a long stone ledge, littered with rocks. Advancing up the cliff were the three heads and shoulders of the Frenchies from the smuggling vessel. Awaiting them at a level between the beach and myself was

Kestrel, hiding behind a rock, with his pistol drawn. My first surge of relief at seeing him was short-lived. A few feet behind Kestrel was Bernard Kemp, also armed and ready for action. But where was Ronald? It took me another minute to decide that the skulking shadow a few yards behind Kemp was Ronald, also armed.

Though cheered to realize help was at hand, the thought occurred to me that Kestrel was unaware of Kemp's presence, while the reverse was not true. Of course, there was Ronald for a backup, but whether he was swift enough to shoot Kemp before Kemp shot Kestrel was a matter of grave doubt. And all the time the Frenchies kept climbing like billy goats up the cliff. A deadly confrontation would occur within minutes if I didn't do something to prevent it.

The scene enacting itself in my head was as sharp as though it were played out on a stage. When the three smugglers reached Kestrel's level, Kemp would walk out with his pistol in Kestrel's back to join his colleagues. Ronald would have to contend with the four of them, for Kestrel would be helpless, if indeed he was still alive at all. Much help I and my little dagger would be, perched ten or twelve feet above the fray. I must draw closer, before the smugglers reached Kestrel. Between a realization of the danger and the great speed required, I moved too hastily. I lost my footing and came careening down the cliff in a shower of stones and pebbles and shrieks. In the resulting commotion, Kemp jumped out to see what was going on, Kestrel turned and drew his pistol on Kemp, then discovered who it was who had landed in so unexpectedly and, for a few seconds, lost his wits.

"Marion!" He bolted forward, forgetful of more important duties, to rescue me. Though gratified at his chivalry, I deeply regretted his rashness.

A few seconds was long enough for Kemp to take

advantage of the interruption. He dragged me up from the rock by my neck and held me in front of him for a shield. I was gasping for breath. In that first instant, taking inventory of my bones for breakage took precedence over anything else. They appeared to be intact, though my hide was thorougly damaged in various places.

Kemp turned a triumphant stare on Kestrel and pulled me toward the edge of the cliff, as though about to push me off. "If you ever want to see this hellion alive again, I suggest you hand me your pistol. Turn the muzzle toward yourself, and give it to me by the handle—very carefully."

Kestrel, wearing a face like a tiger who had just swallowed a live coal, did as he was told.

Kemp now held a pistol in either hand, still carefully hiding himself behind my skirts. By this time, the three smugglers had finished their climb and joined us. Of Ronald there was no sign, but he wasn't the sort to desert his comrades in distress. He would be there, wildly planning some impracticable scheme of rescue.

The ensuing conversation was in French, peppered with gross obscenities. I shall put it into English that anyone might read without blushing, unless an asterisk will set him off. The tallest of the French smugglers spoke for his group. He was a swarthy man with a black toque pulled low over his eyes. His face was merely a blur of ugliness, and his voice was rough.

"What * * * have we here, Kemp?" he asked laughing. "A little * * * for the men?" His oily black eyes examined me at this sally.

When Kemp had Kestrel under control again after his outbreak at this description of me, he replied, "They're welcome to the * * *. You'd be doing England a favor— and France, too—if you'd drop her in the Channel after you * * * her."

I didn't have to wonder whether Kestrel spoke French.

He was once again thrown into a bluster of futile action. I regretted that he should hear me described as * * * flotsam.

"You have the money, and the letter?" the Frenchman asked.

Kemp handed the Frenchie one of his pistols. "Watch the * * *," he said. Then he removed the letter from his inner pocket and handed it over. The satin wrapping had been removed, but the odor of violets lingered. During this transaction, Kemp was careful to keep me between himself and Kestrel. Kestrel hadn't made any successful move yet, but his eyes were alert, wary, waiting for the moment to do something brave, and get us both killed.

The Frenchie and Kemp went on talking a moment about the * * * brandy and the * * * money to be paid for it. Their profanity wasn't limited to me by any means. Had it not been for the other two smugglers, standing as eager for mischief as a pair of foxes in the chicken coop, I am sure Kestrel would have made some move. I know I would have. Having failed in my mission was hard to accept, but having failed, the next order of business was to at least escape alive, and preferably not to escape as the plaything of a band of smuggling rogues. Bad as that would be, I feared Kestrel's fate would be worse. Kemp couldn't let him live to tell tales, and the Frenchies would hardly take an English lord along for their amusement. What they would do was break his neck and push him over the cliff, to wash up as an "accidental" victim of drowning. Our last hope, Ronald, was nowhere in evidence. There hadn't been a sign of him since I fell off the cliff. I sincerely hoped he hadn't gone for help. We'd be only a memory by the time he got back.

On the beach below, the brandy had all been unloaded. It looked like about twenty barrels lined up for delivery. Kemp had handed over the money; the smuggler leader had counted it and passed it to one of his minions to carry. It remained only to decide what to do with Kestrel and myself. They had their heads together, behind my back, talking it over. There was a little disagreement between them. Kemp was all for drowning us both; the Frenchie was less eager to add murder to his crimes. If ever Kestrel was going to make a move, this was the time. I caught his eye and nodded, telling him I was ready to follow his lead. I even remembered my dagger, and managed to get it out of my pocket to show Kestrel. If only Ronald would give us a sign that he stood ready! But no sign came. He had either gone for help, or was waiting for us to make the first move. If he had left, we were dead, so I decided to make the move myself and hope he hopped out from behind the rocks.

It was Kemp who wanted us dead. I didn't think the Frenchies would murder us if Kemp could be disposed of. With this in mind, I got a firm grip on my little dagger, gave Kestrel a nod to show him trouble was coming, and, turning swiftly, plunged the dagger into Kemp's side. He emitted a strangled gasp and fell toward the edge of the cliff—unfortunately, taking me with him. His two hands clutched at my skirts, but I managed to grab his pistol.

Caught off guard, the smugglers stood a moment gaping and cursing, trying to figure out what had happened. Kestrel leapt at the ringleader and got hold of his pistol. The other two weasels took to their heels, shimmying down the rock cliff like the sheep they were.

Ronald appeared, brandishing his pistol dangerously as he flew to my rescue. "Are you all right, Marion?"

"I'm fine. You keep guard on this scoundrel," I said, pointing to Kemp.

The leader of the band broke out into protestations of innocence. "Oh, monsieur, have a pity on a father of four darling daughters. I meant you no harm. My only crime is supplying most excellent brandy to fine English gentlemen.''

"And using language that would shock the devil," I reminded him.

"The letter," Kestrel demanded, holding out a peremptory hand.

The letter was handed over without a single protest. "Merely a billet-doux to Monsieur Kemp's lady friend at Calais, is it not so?" the smuggler asked, with the innocent face of a saint.

Kestrel glanced at the envelope and said he thought not. As the Frenchie appeared to know no English, that was the language I used to confer with Kestrel. "Let him go," I advised. "There are a dozen or so of them on the beach. They might come after us if their chief doesn't join them." A glance below showed this was what the men had in mind. Already they were gathering like vultures for the ascent. "It's Kemp you're after. These smugglers aren't interested in spying. Delivering the letters is only a sideline to them."

Kestrel was no enemy to smugglers, so long as they confined their business to smuggling. He dismissed the ringleader with a warning. "I'll be on the lookout for you. If you show your nose near here again, be prepared to have it blown off."

"Monsieur is most generous. He will be remembered in my prayers. Many thanks to the kind lady." An echo of praise for the kind gentleman and the generous lady trailed behind him as the smuggler disappeared over the edge of the cliff.

"Are you all right, Marion?" Kestrel asked. I rather think that had we been alone, he might have done more than ask. Even with Ronald present, he drew me into his arms and turned my face up to examine a bruise on my cheek with tender interest.

"All tattered and torn, but very much alive," I assured him.

"You were magnificent," he said. The tone was one of surprised admiration, and the voice was husky.

I reluctantly detached myself from his arms and said, "When pushed to the wall, one must do something. Now, what shall we do about this carcass?" I asked, and went to examine Kemp.

I pulled back his cape and other clothing to examine his wound. The presence of a considerable quantity of blood made it appear worse than it was. His layers of clothing had cushioned the dagger's force, so that his wound was not very deep. He wasn't even unconscious, but he was in a sullen mood and didn't say much.

"Does anyone have a clean handkerchief?" I asked.

Ronald's was produced. There was little to be done on a cliffside, so I merely covered the wound with the clean cloth and ripped another strip from my skirt to hold it in place till we could get him to a doctor.

"It will be hard to get a wounded man up that sheer cliff," I pointed out. I wasn't looking forward to getting myself up it, to tell the truth.

"Cliff?" Ronald asked. "Why, there's a staircase cut into the wall about a quarter of a mile farther along. Don't tell me you climbed down that cliff?"

I was filled with chagrin to consider the unnecessary hardship I had undergone. Kestrel and Ronald examined the cliffside, which certainly looked unclimbable from below, exchanging incredulous shakes of their heads at my folly. "I didn't know there was a staircase," I said nonchalantly.

"It's a miracle you weren't killed," Kestrel scolded.

"It's a miracle we all weren't killed. How did you two come to let Kemp get between you? When I saw him sneaking up on you, Kestrel, I decided I'd best come down and help you. Unfortunately, I slipped on the stones. These kid slippers weren't made for mountain climbing."

It was Ronald who answered. "We couldn't find

131

Kemp, but Nick knew the spot where the smugglers landed, and we knew he must be lurking somewhere nearby. He suggested I climb up here and keep a lookout while he walked along the beach, trying to draw him out of hiding. While Nick was farther along the beach, Kemp came climbing up and stationed himself in front of me. I couldn't very well warn Nick when he came back without giving myself away, so Nick just called me a few times, and when I couldn't answer, he hid himself behind a rock, and we both watched and waited.

"You might have had the sense to shoot Kemp when you saw him starting to climb up!" I exclaimed.

"No, Nick wanted to take him alive, to question him, you know, and find out if anyone else is in this game with him. I just waited, ready to jump into action at the first sign of trouble."

"You didn't figure my falling into Kemp's hands was trouble?" I asked.

"Well, of course, but by the time I worked my way forward, he was already hiding behind your skirts. There wasn't much I could do then, with you in the way."

"We'll discuss this later," Kestrel said. "We've got to get Kemp out of here. We need a litter. Would you mind going to Longville Manor for help, Ron?"

"I think we can handle him, between the three of us," Ronald countered.

I looked at Kemp—not a small man—and I considered the distance to the manor. "Think again. Go for help, Ronald."

"Well, come on then," he said, waiting for me to join him.

"I'll stay here, in case Kemp worsens. Bring a doctor if you can rouse one." With a grumble of protest at always having to be the errand boy, Ronald left.

It was not solely solicitude for that rogue, Kemp, that

132

decided me to remain behind with Kestrel. I had sensed a warmth in his regard earlier on, and thought privacy might increase it. When he took my arm and led me a little away from Kemp, I assumed he meant to assure himself I was unharmed, and compliment me on my valor.

Imagine my astonishment when the first words he uttered, and in a pretty rough voice, too, were "I hope this night has taught you the folly of forcing your way into matters that don't concern you. You might have been killed, and got us all killed."

It knocked the wind out of me. For thirty seconds I was speechless. By the time I found my tongue, my temper had flared higher than Kestrel's. "I might have, but I decided to save your worthless life instead! Is this the thanks I get? I'd like to know where you'd be now if I hadn't handled Kemp for you!"

"I would have shaken the truth out of Nel, and arrested Kemp hours ago."

"How did you know about Nel?"

"I saw her go into the library, all dressed for traveling in the middle of the night. I knew Sir Herbert wasn't a traitor, and when I learned he was pressuring her to marry Harcourt, I began to suspect the ninny had done something idiotic. I was watching her. I was about to catch her when I heard you moaning, and had to see what muddle you'd gotten yourself into. She got away from me and of course flew straight to Kemp with the letter. I wasn't sure who her contact was at that time, though of course I suspected Kemp. He fills all my criteria for a spy—penniless, no character. Once Nel was away from me, I had no choice but to come here and see who turned the letter over to the Frenchies."

This didn't seem the auspicious moment to straighten him out on a few details. Instead, I attacked him for his laggardly way of conducting himself under fire. "You didn't even know Kemp was behind you with a pistol at your back. Why do you think I was hurrying down, and lost my footing and fell?"

"Yes, fell right into his hands! That was a marvelous help!"

"More help than you! Who stopped him from killing us all? Tell me that!"

"I could hardly leap at him when he had a pistol at your head. By God, I'm beginning to wish I had. It would take more than a pistol shot to get through that thick skull of yours."

My temper flared out of control. I had put myself in jeopardy for this cretin whose idea of gratitude was insults. I raised my hand and delivered a resounding smack across his cheek. A stunned expression flittered across his face as his head whipped aside with the force of the blow. From the shadows beyond, Kemp let out a chuckle of approval. "I promise you I will not interfere in your bungling efforts to save England again, sir."

I lifted my head and made to stalk off. Before I took a step, Kestrel's hands came out and grabbed my arms. "That's exactly the behavior I've come to expect from you. You have no manners, no sense, no dignity. Your idea of gentility is puffing yourself off, claiming credit for accomplishments not your own."

"My accomplishments are my own, whatever you may have weaseled out of Ronald."

"You make yourself ineligible by such actions as you've undertaken tonight. You might have ended up on that lugger, dragged to France as the hostage of those smugglers."

"They would hardly be less amusing than the company I find myself in at the moment. As to eligibility, marriage is of no interest whatsoever to me. I wouldn't accept an offer from anyone I've met in England thus far. If a gentleman is so sensitive to public opinion he balks at my behavior, then let him keep his distance."

This last speech was said through clenched teeth, in a tone that told my listener what gentleman I spoke of.

"Marion, you're impossible!" he howled.

"My name is Miss Mathieson, and you, sir, are a sheep. Follow the herd, and have nothing to do with such untamed wildlife as I. I will not be dictated to by—"

A blaze of frustration flared over Kestrel's hawkish features. He less resembled a sheep than a wolf as he pulled me into his arms for my second passionate embrace that evening. The kiss started where Kemp's had left off, with the quivering at the base of the skull and the trembling down the spine. From there it flamed into a primitive battle, to see which of us could outdo the other in ardor. I wasn't going to be bested in anything by this man, including passion. As his arms crushed me mercilessly against his chest, I wrapped mine around his waist and squeezed till he was gasping. Every atom of my body participated in the struggle. I responded from the tip of my head to the ends of my toes, especially in the area of lungs and what we genteelly call stomach, but mean our entire inner torso, which felt as though it were afire. I hadn't been so exhilarated since the night I was chased down a mountain by a band of Arabs, intent, I believe, on something similar to what Kestrel seemed to have in mind at the moment. The kiss was beginning to run a little out of control on both our sides. I pulled roughly away and sniffed.

He was still scowling, and so was I. "Just the sort of embrace I would expect from a sheep," I scoffed. "Kemp did much better." On this taunting speech I turned and marched away toward the rock staircase. The walking was easy here, unlike my treacherous ordeal.

"Where are you going?" he called.

"To Longville Manor. I suggest you keep an eye on

135

Kemp. He's not quite dead. He might overpower you yet.''

I couldn't be certain whether the reluctant chuckle came from Kemp or Kestrel. My own gurgle of laughter was much more discreet, a mere ruffle of sound in the throat as I hastened to Longville Manor.

Chapter Eleven

I met Roland and a couple of footmen hurrying down the drive of Longville Manor on my way back. "Did you send for a sawbones?" I asked.

"Yes, he's to meet us at the cliff. Do you want to come along and show him exactly where to go?"

"No, leave one of the footmen there to show him the way," I said, and continued on.

Ronald knew my habit of being in the middle of things, and no doubt found my answer strange. So far as I was concerned, the interesting part of that little spy escapade was over—finis. The final wrapping up of it was for doctors and officials. Let them decide what to do with Kemp. I was in the middle of a much more interesting affair now, one I had no intention of conducting without arranging a new toilette.

I went straight to the kitchen at the Manor and asked for a flagon of wine and a basin of hot water to be delivered to my chamber. The scullery maids were putting the last touch of polish on the kitchen. They would have liked to object, I think, till they got a good look at my condition.

"Lawks a mercy, miss. What happened to you?" one asked.

"I was walking along the cliff, looking at the ocean,

and took a tumble. Is there hot water, or shall I have to wait?''

There were two kettles heating on the dying embers. Rather than waiting for the girls to build up the fire again, I said I would make do with what they had. I carried the wine, the girls the water, and they followed me upstairs at once to arrange a rather meager bath.

"Thank you. I suggest you not retire just yet, girls. There will be some commotion at the Manor this evening. A pot of coffee and perhaps some sandwiches would not go amiss.''

Their eager eyes demanded an explanation. "No doubt Sir Herbert will tell you all about it later,'' I said, and closed the door.

Turning back to my room, I deduced that the Manor had an excellent housekeeper. A nightdress had been laid out for me, and Nel's borrowed gown hung again on a hanger in the clothespress. I pulled what remained of my torn suit off and tossed it into the wastebasket. The bathwater was barely tepid, but I had often bathed in water cold as ice from a stream. It was the multiple abrasions and contusions covering my body that caused the discomfort. None was serious enough to require bandaging, however. With a borrowed shawl, the scrapes on my arm could be concealed. After my bath, I was ready to dress. An evening gown that fit properly would also have been appreciated. Lacking that elegance, I did what I could with Nel's. "What I could" means only arranging the shawl artfully to conceal the loose hang of the gown without bundling myself to resemble a school dame.

With careful arranging, a wave of my blond hair was cajoled into tumbling forward, nearly concealing the bruise at the edge of my eye. When all was done, I stood back and examined this stranger in my mirror. I looked intimidating, even to myself. I was too tall, too haughty, too unfeminine. Where Nel's body bulged, mine only curved, and where hers curved, mine was as flat as a ruler. I drank the wine and considered means of changing my appearance. I lowered the scarf, but a collarbone was hardly likely to throw a gentleman into raptures.

I looked to the bottom of my reticule, where a lady keeps her most closely guarded secrets. There, done up in a moleskin bag, hiding beneath my headache powders, were my last hopes: a small pot of rouge and a stick of kóhl purchased in Constantinople. I discreetly applied the rouge, and very carefully edged my eyes with the stick of black kohl. Ladies of a certain class put it on with a trowel in the east, but I wanted only a touch so light as to resemble the hand of nature. Carefully applied, it enlarges and enhances the appearance of the eyes. When I was finished, I was not elated with the result, but satisfied.

Over another glass of wine, I began planning my strategy. Being the person responsible for Miss Longville's downfall would not endear me to her father, nor to his neighbor and coworker, Lord Kestrel. In fact, the whole country would see me as an ogre, persecuting an innocent young lady, if the two of us had to appear in the witness stand. I had to determine how deeply she was involved in this spying business and, if possible, arrange matters so that Sir Herbert meted out her punishment privately. Locking her up in a convent seemed a fitter punishment than hanging. My hope was that she was Bernard Kemp's pawn, no more.

I went tapping on her door, and found her wide awake, dressed and reading a novel. What she held in her hands, in fact, was the first adventure of Aurelia Altmire, and very pleased she was with it, too. She could hardly put it down when I entered.

"Did you give Bernard my letter?" she asked.

"Yes, I unwittingly delivered the plans you contrived to steal from the courier, Miss Longville," I said coolly.

He mouth fell open and a frown pleated her white brow. "What?" If she was acting, she ought to be on the boards. I could have sworn she didn't know what I was talking about.

"What was in that scented satin bundle was plans destined for a colonel at Dover. They were stolen from the courier who was delivering them from London, to transport to Napoleon. What you have done is treason. Do you know the punishment for treason, Miss Longville? Hanging!" I was as harsh as could be, to make her realize the seriousness of what she had done, intentionally or not. "Hanging for yourself, to say nothing of the shame brought down on your poor father's head. The name of Longville will be infamous throughout the length and breadth of the land."

Her lips trembled, and a tear started in her eyes. "I don't know what you're talking about! Bernard said it was only a letter from his smuggling partner, telling him what time to have his men at the beach! I've often done it before."

"Bernard Kemp is a liar and a traitor. How does he arrange for you to get hold of the letters?"

"A man delivers them to me here at the Manor. I always come home on the weekend—that's when Bernard has time free from work to visit me. Bernard can't have the letters delivered to him, because he's watched by the customs men. When they see him come here, they think he's only courting me."

"Courting you!" I scoffed. "Using you, you simpleton!" My words were harsh, but I was vastly relieved to know her involvement was relatively innocent. I felt there was more to it than just delivering the letters, however. Kestrel had indicated the spies knew when the letters would be delivered. "Does Bernard ask you questions about your father's work?"

"Of course he does. Bernard's not a spy. He's very interested in the campaign against Napoleon. He's al-

140

ways asking me what steps the government is taking. He'd like to be an officer himself, but he doesn't want to leave me." Her ignorant conceit accepted this as gospel.

"Miss Longville, has he ever asked you to open your father's private documents and tell him what's in them?"

"Of course not! That would be quite improper, and I told him so."

"Then he *did* ask!"

"He only mentioned it once. I don't have to read the documents. Papa discusses these things with me. He knows the secrets of the government are safe with me."

Bernard Kemp's strategy was becoming clear. He pumped Nel's brain dry of every word her father told her, and to impress him, she discussed these matters at length with her trusting father. No doubt Bernard discovered when important decisions had been made, and when the documents outlining them would be delivered to the army. He had his cohorts ready to relieve the couriers of their burden. To keep a distance from his French cohorts, Nel was used as an unwitting intermediary. Like her father and neighbors, she saw no harm in giving the Gentlemen a hand, so that was what Bernard told her the letters contained.

"As safe as eggs with a weasel. You are in a great deal of trouble, Miss Longville."

"But I didn't do anything, except deliver Bernard's letters from the smugglers. No one cares about that. Papa has his keg in the cellar."

"You hit me on the head this evening. Were you waiting for the letter then?"

"No, I already had received it ten minutes before. Bernard's friend delivers them through the French door in that study. I was just waiting for an opportunity to leave the house and meet Bernard, but then you came in, and I didn't know who you were. I was afraid you were Papa, watching me. I thought I had heard him in the hall earlier. But when I ran into the hall, it was only Kestrel, and I got away from him.''

By dint of repetition I convinced the half-wit of what she had really been delivering. Her concern was not for what she had cost her country, but for what her father would do. ''Oh, Miss Mathieson, you mustn't tell Papa. I won't do it anymore, I promise. I won't ever see Bernard again. I was beginning to think he wasn't eager to marry me. I heard he was seeing a girl who works at the tavern, but he told me it wasn't so.''

''If you care to see that hedge bird, you'll have to go to jail to do it. He's been arrested tonight.'' I didn't mention his wound. It might be the very thing to reactivate her love.

''Do you think he'll tell everyone about me?'' she asked, staring glassy-eyed.

''Your father might convince him not to do so. It would only make him appear more villainous, to have debauched an innocent young girl, turned her to his vile purposes.''

A question formed on her brow. ''You sound just like Mr. Pruitt,'' she said. This name, unmentioned till now, belongs to Aurelia's guardian. Nel held up the book, smiling. ''I didn't see any harm in meeting Bernard in secret, for Aurelia Altmire, in this book, has to meet her lover clandestinely, and he is the one who rescues her from the French soldiers. The author says a young lady must take her destiny in her own hands. I've read this book three times. It inspired me, Miss Mathieson.''

When the anonymous English lady gave that advice, it was intended for rational creatures only. Who could have foreseen its falling into the hands of morons and being so misinterpreted? ''You must realize, Nel, there is a difference between reality and fiction. You should never flout your father's authority.''

''Aurelia would never allow herself to be forced to

142

marry Mr. Harcourt,'' she said, and burst into tears. "That's the only reason I met with Bernard. I don't want to marry Alfred. I'll run away if he makes me.''

The anonymous author wavered between conviction and expediency. She could not in good conscience urge Miss Longville to capitulate completely. "I'll talk to your papa,'' I promised rashly.

"Miss Mathieson, what do you think the judge will do to me? I won't be put in Bridewell, will I? Perhaps Alfred would be a little better than that,'' she said, looking for my opinion.

"Even Alfred would be a little better than that, but it would not do for you to tell your papa so. And in any case, accepting Alfred doesn't change the fact that you have committed serious crimes. I should stand firm on the matter of Mr. Harcourt, if I were you. Is there no one else? . . .''

She frowned a moment, the tears drying on her cheeks. "Lord Kestrel is handsome,'' she said, musingly.

"He rather reminds me of your papa,'' I said nonchalantly. "The sort of gentleman who would expect to rule you with an iron fist.''

"That's true. Mr. Kidd is much more biddable, I think.''

"But not very well to grass.'' Poor Ronald, he must not be sacrificed to this moonling. He deserved better. "Is there no one in London?''

Now that Bernard was becoming a memory, she began to rhyme off a series of young gentlemen who were "quite handsome'' and "rather amusing'' and "seemed somewhat interested.'' Of course, they hadn't the advantage of farms adjacent to Longville, but surely that could be talked away. "You haven't forgotten you said I could stay with you in London, Miss Mathieson?'' she said, smiling innocently.

"Of course not,'' I replied, with very little enthusiasm. I suggested she go to bed. Without prattling of modesty, I felt I could present her case to her father more convincingly than she could herself. The next thing to be done was to rouse up Sir Herbert, but before doing that, I wanted to see if Kestrel and Ronald had returned yet. The saloon was dark and empty. I lit the lamps and waited. Before long, the tread of boots was heard, and the low murmur of men's voices. I had left the front door on the latch and didn't rise to greet them. They saw the lighted saloon and came in, looking like a pair of poachers in their disheveled clothes and dirty faces.

Kestrel seemed surprised at my renovated condition. "All back in shipshape, eh, Miss Mathieson?" He smiled. "I was afraid you might be hurt after your tumble." That "Miss Mathieson" came as a bit of a shock, after our tangle on the cliffs. I was sure I would be Marion, and before long he would be Nick.

"There's no point wallowing in filth when it is unnecessary. What have they done with Kemp?"

"He's jelly to the marrow of his bones," Ronald announced cheerfully. "He was bleating like a sheep. You would have laughed to hear him apologizing and explaining, Marion, when Nick hit him up about kissing you. He said he thought you were Nel, which explains it. In the dark, he mistook you for a young girl. Naturally, he wouldn't have tried to kiss *you*."

"Any gentleman foolhardy enough to attempt that would soon have his ears singed," Kestrel agreed blandly.

"By jingo, Kemp's lucky she didn't run him through with her dagger again."

"Yes, I can appreciate his good fortune in avoiding that," Nick smiled.

"But what happened to him?" I persisted, to change the direction of the conversation. "Is he in custody?"

"Dr. Lattimer patched him up, and the constable

hauled him off to the roundhouse for tonight," Kestrel replied. "I'll have to give evidence at the trial. What we still have to determine is how he coerced Nel into helping him."

"I've spoken to Nel," I said, and briefly outlined what she had told me. "Kemp didn't mention her name?"

Kestrel was studying my face in a curious way. I feared I had used too lavish a hand with the kohl pencil, though his expression was not at all condemning. "No, I shouldn't think he will. It will only blacken his character further to add that to it."

"That's what I was hoping," I nodded.

"Sir Herbert will get her shackled up with Alfred Harcourt in a hurry, and that will take care of Nel," Kestrel said.

Any agreement between Kestrel and myself was "like angels' visits, short and far between." This patriarchal attitude got my hackles in an uproar. "It is Sir Herbert's insistence she marry that yahoo that caused all the trouble in the first place! She won't have him, Kestrel."

His brows rose, his nostrils flared, and he rose to his feet to glare down at me. "In other words, you've been advising her to disobey her father's commands."

I saw from the corner of my eye that Ronald had crossed his arms and assumed his smile reserved for watching me tackle overbearing foes. "I have agreed with her that she has a right to some say in her own destiny. Why should it be for you and Sir Herbert to force the poor child into marriage with a man she despises? Tell me that! And I'll tell you something else; if her father makes her have him, this little spree will be child's play compared to what will follow. It will be a runaway match with the butcher or a traveling salesman. Let Sir Herbert take her to London, where she can choose a husband for herself—some unexceptionable gentleman. I understand there are plenty of them willing to undertake the role.''

"She's only eighteen years old,'' Kestrel shouted. "She doesn't know what's best for her.''

"She's old enough to know what's worst for her!''

"Harcourt is the logical man. He has an excellent character. He'd take care of Nel.''

"He also has a face like a ram.''

"Such personal comments have no place in this discussion. His farm, a very prosperous estate, runs with Sir Herbert's land for miles. Nel would be right next door to her father, home where she grew up and knows everyone.''

"Yes, all the smugglers and attractive fortune hunters! Why must you men think enlarging an estate the only things that matters?''

"A large estate can be run more efficiently. It's more prosperous.''

"The Longvilles are prosperous enough. You and Sir Herbert can bend Nel's ears till the sheep come home, but you won't find her so biddable as you hope. She has a mind of her own.''

"No, Miss Mathieson, she has a piece of *your* disordered mind, which has no more conception of what is proper than one of those sheep you so frequently deride. She would never have had the gumption to challenge her father without your troublesome assistance. You have already made my life a hell. Isn't that enough mischief for one day?''

I opened my lips to answer this charge, but before I could get a word in, he ranted on, a fierce light gleaming in his pale eyes. "And furthermore, Kemp let out that it was you who delivered the letter tonight, not Nel.''

"She told me it was only a note explaining why she couldn't meet him. It seemed preferable to having her

146

slip out again after we'd left. I expect Ronald told you we had already stopped her once.''

''What you should have done was told Sir Herbert. He would have locked her in her room till she came to see reason.''

''No, she would have opened the window and climbed out, if she had her wits about her.'' I began to sympathize with Nel. I hadn't realized how insufferably overbearing and patronizing men could be. But I think what made her behavior in not wanting to marry Harcourt so heinous in the quivering nostrils of Kestrel was that I was involved in it.

''It's obvious you grew up without the proper guidance of a strict father,'' he sneered, ''nor with any guidance at all but your own headstrong stubbornness.''

Any slur on my father was not to be borne. ''My father, sir, was an officer and a gentleman. Not a bloated, conceited oaf like you and Sir Herbert! I never fully appreciated the vastness of your arrogance till tonight. You haven't even spoken to Sir Herbert! If you keep your oar out, I believe I can convince him to turn Harcourt off.''

''Sir Herbert is my friend, and as you have got both oars in the water, you may be sure I shan't keep my tongue between my teeth.'' On that fine mixing of metaphors, he jutted his chin out and glared.

Ronald stood up, ready to appease us both. ''It seems you two are at right angles over this. I think—''

''When did you begin doing that?'' I demanded.

Having thoroughly offended both gentlemen, I rose like a fury and stomped from the room. At the doorway I turned and leveled a parting shot over my shoulder. ''And furthermore, I have offered Nel shelter in London with me if her father doesn't see reason in this matter. You may tell Sir Herbert so. Come along, Ronald, we must make plans for an early departure tomorrow.''

''Ronald will be required to give testimony at the

trial,'' Kestrel called after my fleeing form. Nuisance! And not a second later it occurred to me that I was more deeply involved than Ronald. Why was I not asked to give testimony? It was because of my sex, of course. The judge wouldn't take the word of a mere female seriously. Spying and such life-and-death matters were men's work. And a fine botch they'd all made of it!

I went to my room but left my door ajar, to hear if Sir Herbert was sent for. I meant to get in the first word if he was. It seems they were letting the poor soul have the last decent night's sleep he'd have for many a long moon. I could almost pity the man, if I weren't so vexed with him. Many troubles assailed me as I sat waiting for Ronald to come up and we could discuss the matter. Not least of them was my rash offer to house Nel. I truly didn't want the ninny cluttering up my apartment. I was in the middle of my lecture tour, too, which meant either dragging her along with me, or hiring a chaperone for her.

I was due to speak at Canterbury tomorrow night, and I had no cash with me to arrange transportation there. My belongings were scattered across the countryside. My trunk of memorabilia now at the inn at Redden, my necklace at the shoemaker's, my Aurelia manuscript hopefully still unsold at Chatham, and Ronald's watch at Ashford. I felt a sting of remorse, too, that some of Aurelia's advice to impressionable young ladies was open to misinterpretation.

And after I had pondered all these nagging trifles, I was left with the more distressing realization that Kestrel thought me as freakish as a bearded lady. That embrace on the cliffside had been born of frustration, not love. He was a conservative gentleman who would marry his next-door neighbor, providing her papa had a large farm touching his. There was no romance in his soul. He would be exactly the wrong husband for me. I didn't intend to have my activities trammeled by a domineering husband too concerned for what people thought. I couldn't possibly live under such confining strictures, and worse yet, I wasn't going to have the opportunity to refuse. It was best to forget him, and get on with my life.

It was a pretty good life. After the war, I'd go to the Continent and research another serious book. There was a world of history and legend in Greece, for instance. I hadn't begun to scratch the surface of Greece. How thrilling to dip into the classics, and go to see with my own eye where civilization was born.

This was the thought I took to bed with me an hour later, when still Ronald had not come up, nor Sir Herbert gone down. It was very hard to concentrate on Greece when my heart lay heavy in my chest. I had really thought Kestrel was coming to care for me. When had I decided I loved him? Was this love, this gnawing ache inside, and not the rapturous flights of ecstasy so generously bestowed on Aurelia? If so, I wanted no part of it. Whatever joy it might bring, it was too dearly bought.

Chapter Twelve

It was necessary to resort to an old trick learned from Ishmael Aga, chief of the Delibash tribes, to achieve any sleep at all that night. He suffered from insomnia, and to court Lethe, he used to mentally design arabesques, intricate interlacing swirled patterns used as decoration on everything in the East. After an hour, my imagination had filled the ceiling above me with these complex knots, but my mind was as unsettled as ever. As a result of my bad night, I overslept the next morning. When I finally awoke, I was very thoroughly disgruntled and more tired than when I went to bed. I was ready to take on Sir Herbert and Lord Kestrel and anyone else who looked at me aslant. I went storming downstairs to do battle with the world, and found only Ronald in the breakfast room, huddling over a cup of coffee.

"Where is everyone?" I demanded.

He gave me a disparaging look. "There's no point mounting your high horse, Marion. Everything's been taken care of. Nick and Sir Herbert have gone to Hythe to speak to the lord-lieutenant and explain away Nel's innocent involvement. Nick talked Sir Herbert out of mentioning that you actually delivered the letter."

"Kind of him! When was all this arranged, and why was I not invited to be present?"

"Nick didn't want you here, rubbing Sir Herbert the wrong way. We settled most of it last night after you were asleep."

"It may interest you to know I did not sleep last night. I was awake forever, and didn't hear Sir Herbert come downstairs."

"We didn't send for Longville till after one in the morning. Nick and I thrashed out what had best be done first. We had him come down the servants' stairs so as not to disturb you."

"To prevent my having an opportunity to make him see reason, you mean. That weasel! Next you will tell me they've already married Nel off to Alfred Harcourt."

"No, Nel's future was all tied up this morning. She took breakfast with us. She isn't going to marry Harcourt. She's going to visit her cousin in Bath. A letter's already been sent to the cousin to come and fetch her."

"We'll see about that! Packing her off to some ogre to trim her into line. I offered Nel shelter with me, and I mean to see she gets it!"

"She is delighted to be going to her cousin. It seems Mrs. Fitzroy is a great favorite of hers. She has a son—not terribly well to grass, but what Nick called 'a bright lad.' He's very keen on raising sheep," Ronald added, with a knowing look. "Sir Herbert is going to resign his commission with the government and come home to tend his farm. I expect within a few months, he'll have a son-in-law to assist him."

"At least they aren't making her marry Harcourt."

"We have Nick to thank for that. He explained his views to Sir Herbert with a generous strength. The words 'bloated, conceited oaf' were used at one point. I think you went a bit too far there, my girl. Outdid yourself. Sir Herbert didn't take kindly to it, but Nel cleverly went into a fit of bawling and defended her papa, which did a world of good. Blamed her rash behavior on some novel she'd been reading. Sir Herbert was determined to push the match forward at first, but between Nel's tears and Nick's tongue-lashing, he was talked out of it.''

"I'm surprised to hear Kestrel changed his opinion.''

"So was I, to tell the truth. Last night after you left he went into a fine rant, practically vowing that he'd see Nel married to Alfred if it killed him. It sounded like spite to me—and he has no reason to spite Nel.'' His sapient look wasn't needed to tell me the object of this tender emotion. "By this morning he had calmed down and actually urged Sir Herbert to be lenient with the girl. A marriage without love would only lead to strife, he said.''

"Well then, some good came of my hysterics.'' I went to the sideboard and filled my plate. My temper was beginning to calm down as I considered Ronald's news. It was actually a relief to know Nel wouldn't be battened on me, so long as she wasn't being made to have Harcourt. Kestrel was apparently calming down, too. I was interested to hear if he might have said anything about me, but didn't quite care to enquire directly. I went at it by indirection instead.

"Did Sir Herbert say when he would be back?'' I didn't suppose for a minute that he would return without Kestrel.

"No, but I should think he'd be here by noon.''

That didn't leave me much time to gather my belongings up from around the countryside and get to Canterbury in time for the lecture. "That late?'' Possibly Kestrel would return earlier.

"We don't have to wait for them. I told Sir Herbert about your lecture this evening, and he offered the loan of a carriage and team to take care of our errands. It was kind of him, but I suspect the truth is, he just wanted to get you out of the house. Nel was quoting your advice freely. 'Miss Mathieson said' came out in

152

every other sentence. Sir Herbert particularly ordered Nel not to leave her room till we were gone, and requested that you not go to her. I gave him my word, Marion,'' he added, and looked at me hopefully.

I was rapidly losing interest in Sir Herbert and his daughter. ''Then it seems I shall just have to steal Nel's gown, and not have the pleasure of saying good-bye to them or Kestrel,'' I said, and peered to see if Ronald had anything to say about Nick.

''You can leave a note, and return Nel's gown later,'' he suggested. ''Pity you have to be seen in public in it, with those red slippers.''

''Why should I bother with a note? If rude dismissal is the order of the day, I shan't put myself to the trouble. And I'll give this gown to the first servant girl I meet. What will happen to Bernard Kemp and his band of merry men?''

''Nothing will happen to the Gentlemen, except they'll require a new leader. No one's pursuing their involvement. In fact, they weren't involved in the spying, only smuggling, and that's considered an honorable profession here on the coast. Kemp will be prosecuted for the traitor he is.''

''All's well that ends well then, as Mr. Shakespeare said.'' The ending was not quite what I could wish, but it was the end of our adventure all the same. ''You might as well go and see to the carriage, Ronald, as you've finished breakfast. We shall be leaving in approximately half an hour. This gammon is delicious,'' I added blandly. Actually, it might have been tanned leather for all the heed I paid to it.

As soon as Ronald left, I pushed my plate away, hardly touched, and sat sipping coffee. When a servant came to see if I wanted anything, I started from a fit of the dismals to enquire ever so offhandedly whether Lord Kestrel had left me a message. He had not. ''What time did he and Sir Herbert leave this morning?'' I enquired.

153

"An hour ago, ma'am. Would you like to leave a message for them?"

The whole staff knew I had been hinted away. This being the case, I would sooner ride a tiger than try to cajole Kestrel with a polite note. I answered testily, "No, I would not. This coffee is very bitter and quite cold."

"Shall I make a fresh pot, ma'am?"

"I haven't time to wait for that. I shall be leaving almost immediately." I rose while she still stood there with her mouth open, and marched to my room.

If the ninny thought she would receive a pourboire when I left, she was very much mistaken. I took no formal leave of anyone, but just threw on my bonnet and pelisse to wait belowstairs for the carriage. Ronald soon joined me. He didn't look any too perky either.

"You're regretting that you'll have to return here for the trial, I expect?" I said, giving his arm a sympathetic pat.

"Nick said it won't be for a couple of weeks. I shan't mind that. What's troubling me is that I don't like setting out on a trip without any money," he said. "I should have bitten Sir Herbert's ear for some blunt before he left."

"I'm glad you mentioned it. We'll stop at Hythe and see if something can be arranged."

"It would be better to wait till we get to Canterbury. No one knows you in Hythe—they might be reluctant to forward you funds. In Canterbury you'll be known because of the lecture."

"That would make eminent sense if we were going directly to Canterbury, but we're not. We're going to Redden to pick up my trunk for the lecture and to Chatham to look for my Aurelia notes, and to Ashford to give that mawworm a piece of our minds for selling us an ornamental pistol and to get your watch back. We can do it all and still be in time for the lecture if we get an early start.''

Ronald lifted a knowing brow. ''The fact that Nick is in Hythe has nothing to do with it, I suppose?''

''I'll give him a last blast if we happen to run into him.'' I waited to hear if Ronald had anything more to say on the subject of Kestrel.

''There's the carriage. Let's go.''

''Oh dear! We haven't made any arrangement to return the horses Kestrel hired for us yesterday. We can't leave them here, Ronald.''

''Nick's going to look after them.''

I had run out of excuses. If we didn't meet Kestrel in Hythe, I would never see the wretched man again, and I didn't know whether I was happy or sad. The bank manager at Hythe knew precisely who I was. Word of our escapade had already begun circulating through the little seaside town. A house guest of Sir Herbert Longville's was given fifteen pounds credit with no difficulty. There wasn't a sign of Kestrel in the town, and so we left. I peered over my shoulder till the carriage made the first bend, then decided to put this incident behind me.

We retraced yesterday's journey, recovering Ronald's watch, then on till we reached Chatham. A trip to the bookstall where he had discovered Cooke's book of devotions saw me in possession of the first three chapters of Aurelia's new adventures, and a pound out of pocket for the leather lap case, but I was happy to have it back. It was a constant companion on all my travels.

I opened it and pretended to read over my manuscript as we went on to Redden. It gave me privacy to think without interruption from Ronald. There is no secret what was in my thoughts—Lord Kestrel. Perhaps if I hadn't been so hot in Nel's defense last night, I would be with him now. Surely that kiss in the moonlight had been more than a caprice on his part.

My mind settled on that embrace, and I idly jotted down a few phrases that might be useful when Belvoir rescued Aurelia from the highwaymen. "The pressure of his lips on hers caused a fire to flame within her" came to mind. "She felt she had entered a celestial paradise of eternal bliss." But this was mere verbiage. It hadn't been like that at all. Euphemism and allegory and eternity had nothing to do with it. It was an immediate sensation, very much centered in the pit of the stomach, and the here and now. It was a wild beating of the heart, a raw hunger, more closely attuned to animal needs than some evanescent paradise. I hadn't been so shaken and so vitally alive since the night Ronald and I faced Prince Nasar's rebellion.

"What are you doing?" Ronald asked.

I crossed out those polite lies and uttered a new one. "Just thinking about the lecture tonight."

"Do you miss Nick?" he asked.

My look was rebukeful, but I decided to answer. "I am delighted to be free of him. I never met such a pompous, egotistical man in my life."

"He's not so bad when you get to know him."

"I believe I know him as well as you do, Ronald."

He just smiled in his hateful, knowing way. "I miss Nel," he said. "She was very pretty. One of those vulnerable girls a fellow would like to cherish."

"Milksop!" I charged. Then we both fell silent.

I got my gold necklace from the cobbler at Redden before we went to the inn. Mr. Monahan had our cases safely stowed away. We took lunch there, thanked him profusely, tipped him, and were off to Canterbury. There was a moment of weakness when I thought of redeeming Kestrel's emerald ring as an excuse to see him again, but I didn't have enough money. Really, that is all that prevented me. I asked Monahan to keep it safely. To keep my mind from less useful matters, I regaled Ronald with my speech as we went to Canterbury. I playfully inserted an addition relating to his part in the Arab uprising in the desert. He smiled sheepishly.

"Well, it's true, Marion. I was the one who confronted Prince Nasar."

"It isn't true that I'm 'well over thirty,' or that Mr. Lambert was a fish merchant. He had a whole fleet of fishing ships."

"I only said that to discourage Nick. You don't want someone like Kestrel dangling after you, complaining about your doings. I wondered when he mentioned that bit about your views on marriage. I believe he was becoming interested in you, but never fear, I nipped that in the bud."

"Thank you," I said. As the subject was in the air, I ventured a question. "He didn't say anything this morning before he left? Anything about me, I mean?"

"Oh, I forgot to tell you!"

"What?" I nearly jumped from my seat for joy.

"He said to thank you for your help, he hoped the lecture went well, and . . . what was the other?" I sat holding my breath till he continued. "Oh yes, he said to say good-bye."

"Oh."

Conversation dwindled to silence, till Ronald decided I should run once more through the part about Prince Nasar and the revolt, to make sure his heroics got full play.

Evening was falling by the time we reached Canterbury. We drove along Westgate Street, passing many fine churches along the way. The whole city was quite impressive, with a library, museum, and guildhall. We hadn't time to visit the famous cathedral, but after a short sight-seeing tour of the place, went straight to our hotel. Our reservations were at the Rose, in High Street.

We went directly to our rooms, where I sent my gown down to be pressed for the evening; also my oriental costume. My publisher, Mr. Oates, had urged me to wear the oriental outfit, but I thought the illustration in my book gave a good idea of how it looked on. As Ronald and I ate dinner in my room, however, I decided I would wear it that night after all. Many members of the London audience had expressed regret that they couldn't see it in action.

"That's a trifle farouche, isn't it?" Ronald objected when I told him my decision.

"I'm a farouche creature. It seems I'm already an oddity. I might as well be a truly outrageous one." What difference did it make? I had set myself beyond the pale of marriage. Why not go whole hog and really give the provincials something to gape at? As Oates so genteelly put it, "It'll get you ink in the journals, and sell books."

Ronald left after dinner, and I dressed myself before the mirror. The long scarlet satin vest had broad sleeves open to the elbow. Over it went my silk jacket embroidered in gold. The trousers of yellow were loose, falling in folds and tight at the ankles. A pair of embroidered Moroccan leather shoes without heels, turned up at the toe, were slipped on, and last came the turban. It was a large, ceremonial affair, held together in the front by a bright brooch. If one could overlook the strangeness of the outfit, I think one would admit it was strikingly attractive. Not for everyone, of course, but my height and proud carriage could wear it. I hung my abba loosely over my shoulders, planning to remove it for the lecture. When riding through the desert, I was used to wearing a sash to hold my dagger and pistol, but I would not mar the splendor of my outfit with those accoutrements tonight. Those and other paraphernalia were fastened up in my case, which Ronald would carry for me.

Ronald, who had seen me attired as I was that night any number of times, was strangely loath to go down into the lobby with me. "I'll have the carriage pick us up in the alley," he offered. "That way, you won't have to be seen in the hotel."

"I am not averse to being seen. The outfit might cause some of the hotel clients to attend the lecture."

"Yes but—but everyone will stare, Marion! You won't be at all comfortable."

"By which you mean *you* will not be comfortable. If you've developed a set of sensitivities since coming home, by all means slink out the kitchen door like a scullery maid. I shall depart through the lobby."

He sighed, fastened the abba tightly around me to conceal as much as possible of my outfit, and we left. There was no shortage of stares as we strode grandly out to our carriage. A pair of spinsters jumped back as though I might pull out a brace of pistols and shoot them. "I didn't know there was a traveling fair in town!" I heard one exclaim. One bold rogue enquired where I kept my elephant. "Why, I thought you were it!" I answered sharply. He was a large man, which made the retort less pointless than it sounds.

On the street a crowd appeared from nowhere, pointing and gaping as though I were a freak from Bartholomew Fair. It was a relief to climb into the carriage and close the door behind us.

"I'll go to the room and get your gown if you want to change before the lecture," Ronald offered. "If you're having second thoughts about wearing the trousers, I mean."

"I have not changed my mind. There is nothing improper in this outfit. It covers more of my anatomy than half the gowns you may see at any polite party anywhere, including Canterbury. You sound like the veriest hick, Ronald. One would not think you have been halfway round the world."

"But we're home now. These are English people we'll

be meeting tonight. You know how . . . traditional they are.''

''Narrow-minded is the word you're looking for. Part of the reason I wrote my book is to show Englishmen how other people live. Well, other people, other human beings, dress like this.''

''Even in the desert, those are men's clothes,'' he insisted.

''Men, women—what's the difference? We're all people. You remember the men at Palmyra wore those funny petticoats, trimmed up with leather and beads and blackamoor's teeth and I don't know what all. They jingled like tinkermen when they walked.''

''We're back in civilization now.''

''Rome was civilized, wouldn't you say? The Roman senators wore skirts. I can wear trousers.''

''Hail Caesar,'' Ronald said weakly, then pulled his head back from the window so he wouldn't be seen driving with me as we began the trip to the lecture hall.

Chapter Thirteen

The opening we had found most impressive was for Ronald to go onto the stage first and give me a buildup. When the hall was quiet and the audience eager to hear me, I walked onto the stage. You would have thought I was naked as the day I was born to hear the gasp of astonishment at my trousers. The gasp was followed by a thrilling ripple of high-pitched chatter. I had expected some reaction, but hardly this degree of shock. I held my breath, afraid that someone would start jeering or throwing vegetables at me. There was something dreadfully like a snicker starting up in the rear section, where the less costly seats are. I kept my head high, my shoulders erect, and stared boldly into the featureless sea of faces. The hall was full to the doors. I took a deep breath and made a salaam, an Oriental sign of welcome which consists of touching the palm of the right hand against the forehead while bowing deeply. It means "Peace be upon you." I began speaking immediately while I could be heard over the snickers. The most dreadful foreboding took hold of me that I would be hooted off the stage.

"Can you do the Indian rope trick?" one ignoramus shouted, to a scattered burst of laugh.

"Do you ride a horse or a magic carpet, lady?" soon was hurled at me.

I stood still, appalled, wondering if I should leave the stage. Fortunately, some gentleman in the audience came to my rescue. Over the headlights I dimly perceived a black jacket rise from his seat and go to that troublesome rear section. He bodily lifted one lout from his seat and kicked him out the door. This had the salutary effect of quieting the others. I rushed into my lecture at once.

"Thank you for coming to hear me this evening, ladies and gentlemen. Before I begin my talk, I would like to point out to you the names of the various vestments I am wearing, and explain how it comes that I, an English lady, stand before you in an abba and a pair of shalwars." So saying, I removed the abba and handed it to Ronald, who continued sharing the stage with me. I was thankful for his dignified presence. I thought calling the trousers by their foreign name might mitigate the offense of wearing them, and obviously some explanation for the clothing was required, before I was faced with a riot.

I believe I did the right thing to confront the matter of the trousers head-on. The snickerers were hushed by the more intelligent members of the audience, which gave me time to win the others over. From the clothes I proceeded quickly to display some of the more interesting objects. This had the double advantage of occupying the less educated patrons with something they could understand, and keeping Ronald close by me. We showed them pistols, various swords and daggers, the nargileh—a long-stemmed oriental pipe. I had planned to smoke it myself, but it seemed wise to let Ronald do the honors.

By this time, the snickerers had fallen silent, and I was able to get into the gist of it. Before long, I had them all in the palm of my hand. I spoke of the various climates and seasons, the desert and mountains, giving some idea of the vegetation. There was a ripple of surprise when I described the oaks and firs encountered in the mountains. I was a little surprised myself upon first seeing them. It was the more exotic plants that I dwelt on, of course. The pomegranates and figs and watermelons.

My trip to Palmyra in a Tartavan proved a great success. How the ladies smiled to hear I had been put inside a wire cage like an enormous bird cage for my own safety! Our shipwreck off Rhodes and Ronald's handling of the Prince Nasar rebellion were other highlights. Through it all, there wasn't a peep out of the snickerers in the back row. You know when an audience is with you, and I knew that this lot were entranced. I felt secure that the books would be snapped up in good numbers. After an hour's talk, I mentioned my book was available at the local bookstores, and threw the meeting open for questions. Oates wanted the books at the lecture, but I felt it would be infra dig to peddle my wares myself.

It was extremely interesting to notice the different questions put forward by the two sexes, and to observe that the gentlemen preferred to address themselves to my secretary. With the gentlemen, it was all a discussion of land and wars, religion and politics and farming, whereas the ladies wanted to know how food was prepared, and how the ladies were treated, and where I bathed. I made short shrift of that last subject, but raised an unintentional laugh when I mentioned having to hide my toothbrush from the Mohammedans because of its hog bristles. Eventually it was over. The audience clapped loud and long. I curtsied, Ronald bowed, and we repaired to a little room set aside for our private use.

"That didn't go too badly!" I congratulated myself. "I was afraid there at the beginning that it would be pandemonium."

"I think it might have been if Kestrel hadn't kicked that roisterer in the back row out of the hall."

"Kestrel!"

I stared as if he had said the Prince Regent. "Ronald, you're not saying he was in the audience! He saw me in trousers! Thank God I didn't smoke the nargileh!"

"How could you miss him? I'm certain it was Nick who settled that man's hash. He spoke to the ushers as well to quell any other outbreak. You were preoccupied with your speech, I daresay."

"I didn't know it was him," I said weakly. I was glad I hadn't, or I wouldn't have been able to get a word out of my mouth. My throat felt dry just knowing he had been there, seeing people laugh at me.

The next thought to enter my head was that he might come around to speak to me. To stand on a stage in trousers and a turban was one thing. I had no wish to confront Lord Kestrel at closer range in the outfit. I was acutely aware now of its oddness. I felt not only bizarre but squalid.

"We'll return to the hotel at once," I said.

"I expect Nick might want to speak to us."

"That's exactly why we're leaving."

Even as I said the words, there was a tap at the door. If only some kind deity would turn me into a bird so I could sprout wings and fly out the window!

"That's probably him now," Ronald smiled, and opened the door. "Be nice to him, Marion. If you don't rip up at him, he might put in a word with Castlereagh. I should like to have a go at Boney."

It was indeed Kestrel, decked out in an elegant black evening suit, with an immaculate white shirt gleaming at his throat. Being a well-bred gentleman, he tried valiantly to keep his lips steady and his eyes in their sockets as he stared at my outfit. Once already that evening I had held my head high and spoken boldly when I was trembling in my little moroccan leather slippers with

164

the turned-up toes. I took a deep breath and did an encore.

"Lord Kestrel! What a pleasant surprise!" I said. "What brings you here? I was sure you were still at Hythe taking care of business."

"The business at Hythe was taken care of this morning. I am now on my way to London to report to Castlereagh."

Canterbury, I need hardly remind you, is not en route to London from Hythe, but fifteen miles out of the way. This seemed an occasion when a lady need not be too clever about geography, however.

"As you invited me to hear your lecture, I stopped off."

"Invited you?" I asked.

"You did say that if I was interested in your travels, I should attend your lecture this evening. I find I am—interested," he said. A small glow lit his eyes, a smile curved his lips as, with an impatient glance at Ronald, he moved closer. The glow, the smile, the impatient glance hinted at an interest in more than my travels. My face, which has remained unstained under the lecherous stare of desert chieftains, chose that moment to blush.

Ronald stood ready to defend me by diverting the discussion to himself. "How did you enjoy the talk, Nick?"

"Very much."

"It was kind of you to handle those louts in the back row," he said.

"Very kind," I added.

Ronald was ready to monopolize the conversation. "A pack of hyenas like that can ruin a lecture. I expect it was Marion's strutting out in trousers that did the mischief. I tried to talk her out of it. They're well enough in the East, but she shouldn't wear them in a Christian country like England."

"If God had meant ladies to wear trousers, he would have given us two legs, like you gentlemen," I replied. "Why don't you take the case to the stage and collect up our artifacts, Ron? We must be getting back to the hotel."

"I'll see Miss Mathieson home," Kestrel added.

Nick looked a bright question at me. "I'll join you shortly at the Rose," I told him.

Ronald left, and Kestrel spoke up quickly to get away from the subject of trousers and travels. "I thought you might be interested to hear how things turned out back at the Manor."

"Ronald explained matters to me this morning."

We discussed the disposition of Kemp and Nel for a moment, but as he had nothing new to add, that topic soon died, and I said, "It's been a fatiguing day. I should like to go back to my room now, if you please."

"Yes, of course." He held my abba, making no move to turn it into an intimate gesture, but just dropping it on my shoulders. The abba was the least fantastic part of my ensemble. It wasn't so very different from our English pelisse. Other than the silk tent erected on my head and the Moroccan slippers, I now looked fairly normal. I would gladly have replaced the turban with a bonnet had I had one with me. But I had not, so we left.

Kestrel's sleek black coach with a lozenge on the door awaited us. The crowd in front of the assembly hall behaved better than I expected when they saw the style of my escort. Kestrel's majestic gaze kept them from any overt rudeness. His liveried footman suited in dark green hopped to open the door. The fellow stood with his mouth hanging open till Kestrel asked him if he had swallowed a bee. I felt very like Aurelia in one of her more pampered moments as I slid onto the soft squabs of the banquette. Kestrel didn't sit across from me as I anticipated, but on the seat beside me. My heart was not wildly beating, but it fluttered erratically. Aurelia would have thrown herself on her hero's chest and thanked him tearfully for saving her honor at the lecture.

The anonymous English lady sat stiff as a ramrod, desperately seeking something unemotional to say. "You should stop at Redden and recover your emerald ring. I asked Monahan to hold it for you when I picked up my trunk."

"I've already sent a footman after it."

"You mentioned making your report to Castlereagh, Kestrel."

He reached out in the darkness and grasped my hand. "Don't you think you might call me Nicholas, Marion?"

The fluttering heart began throbbing, but the voice was as flat as water on a platter. "Certainly, if you like. What I had in mind was that you might put in a good word for Ronald and myself. We are still interested in assisting with the sort of work you do."

"Would your lecture circuit permit it? How heavily are you booked up?"

"I only give one lecture a week, and could always postpone it a day or two if a more interesting job offered. The lectures are mere publicity. I actually spend most of my time writing."

"Writing what? I thought you had already written up your trip."

"I—I'm writing a—a novel now."

"I see. Something on the order of the book I picked up at Chatham, is it? Like the author of that novel, you spent time in the Peninsula and could—" He came to a conscious stop. In the darkness of the carriage there was a gasp of surprise as he turned to study me.

"Something of that sort, I daresay, though I haven't read any of those books. An adventurous romance to amuse ladies in their spare hours is what I am writing."

A knowing chuckle rumbled in this throat. "Here I have been picturing you as an invincible Amazon, unaware of such maidenly pursuits as blushing and having vapors. I was half-afraid to confront you tonight. I thought you'd throw a dagger in my back. Had I realized you are steeped in romance, I wouldn't have let you leave the manor. Tell me, Marion, which do you *really* prefer? Battling emirs yourself or having hysterics on velvet sofas, while a host of gentlemen draw swords to defend you?"

"I can't imagine what you're talking about."

"I should have seen it long ago. The style of writing is not that different. Both books are lurid—vividly colored and highly romanticized."

"The difference being that *my* book is fact, not fiction!"

"The major difference, Marion, is that you are ashamed of making public your daydreams. Aren't we all protective of our private thoughts, to some degree? I confess I pitched myself into the role of Aurelia's rescuer with the greatest pleasure—but that was between the page and myself."

"You're no Lord Belvoir, I assure you."

"Quite sure you haven't read it?"

"I scanned a few pages. Ronald has a copy."

"Ronald *wrote* the fair copy. That's why you require a secretary!"

My rising anger broke. "What of it?" I demanded sharply. "We are discussing my working for Lord Castlereagh. What I dream or write or don't write is irrelevant. Will you put in a good word for us?"

"He'd never allow a lady to do such dangerous work."

"If that isn't just like a man! I've seen more action than any of his couriers. He had to bribe you to get you to do the work."

"That is not quite accurate. I just made Castlereagh think so for political reasons. Actually, I like the work."

"Well, I would like it, too. I don't want to wait out this war in some corner of a genteel drawing room. I've been dodging bullets since I was a child. Papa took me on all his campaigns, but just because I wear a skirt, no man would consider me fit for any excitement or adventure."

"We cherish the illusion that ladies are to be protected, not put at unnecessary risk. I won't have you mixing with spies and assassins. I wouldn't have a moment's peace."

"*You* won't have me do it? What have *you* to say to anything?" I would like to relate that this was asked in a tone of pique, but I fear the tone was more Aurelia-like than that. A definite tremor warbled in my throat.

Nick's fingers tightened on mine. "I know your aversion to marriage, Marion, but there comes a time in a lady's life when she should think of the future."

"I'm not that old!" I assured him.

Ever the gentleman, Nick promptly changed the subject. "I know I have no right to ask it of you, but I wish you would not involve yourself in any more dangerous business. I'm not the sheep or the slave of public opinion you take me for. I have no objection to the trousers and the lectures—I have decided I can put up with that—but when Kemp held that pistol at your back last night, I nearly had an attack of the vapors."

"I was a little frightened myself," I admitted, and waited with bated breath to hear why his objection, or lack of it, to my mode of dress should be spoken of.

Kestrel said nothing, but his head in the darkness began to descend slowly toward mine. The turban was definitely in the way. I reached up and removed it. With a preening gesture I fluffed my hair out, for the turban crushes it mercilessly.

"Shall I try to improve on last night's performance?"

he asked softly. "Like everything else about me, my kiss failed to satisfy. I believe I could do better now that I realize you are indeed fearless.'

"You could hardly do worse," I encouraged.

He crushed me to him and, to my astonishment, improved on last night's performance. It was a violently ruthless embrace. Aurelia would have been shocked. I felt stirring sensations in parts of my body whose existence I had been unaware of. Wildly beating doesn't begin to do justice to what happened to the heart. Throbbing and pounding were closer to it, like the waves beating the rocks the night I was shipwrecked. I clung to Nicholas as though he were a refuge in this tumultuous storm, but the harder I clung, the higher the waves rose. Waves of surcharged feelings inundated me, drowned me in dangerous passion that promised a good substitute for other dangers.

Not that I mean to say I abandoned my original notion of turning spy. After the more violent waves had ebbed to manageable proportions and we got around to verbal lovemaking and the proposal, I remembered it. There's more than one way to skin a cat. If Castlereagh wouldn't hire a lady, her husband might be more biddable, especially when he has made the gross tactical error of telling her he cannot live without her.

When we went to the Rose an hour or so later, Ronald was pacing the floor, worrying what had happened to me.

"Ronald, you'll never guess what!" I exclaimed.

He took one look at our smiling faces and said, "Oh yes I will. You're engaged."

"That, too, but we're going to help Nick with his spying work!"

Nick held his head in his hands and made a grimace. "I must have been mad!" he howled.

"When?" Ronald asked.

"Very soon. We thought perhaps after Marion's next lecture," Nick told him.

"He means when can we start work," I explained to my fiancé, who looked taken aback to learn what took precedence with Ronald. I shan't add "and me." It would be impossible to judge which victory was more thrilling.

"One never knows when the next job will come up," Nick said.

"We'll leave for London early tomorrow morning," I decided. "We'll want to be on hand if a job comes up suddenly. We don't want it going to someone else."

"I thought you might like to go to my estate at Margate and await me there," Nick suggested.

"What, and sit looking at a herd of sheep all day long?"

"I could join you in a day or two. You could make the wedding arrangements and rest up—recover from your recent ordeal."

"What ordeal?" Ronald asked, blinking in confusion.

"The ordeal of committing myself to marriage," I told him. "Now that I am starting into my thirties, I think it is time to settle down." Ronald and Nick exchanged a laughing look. "Till after the war at least. Then we'll go on an extended honeymoon, Nick. I have been thinking a deal of Greece recently."

"Yes, by Jove, I'm looking forward to that," Ronald agreed.

Nick opened his mouth and said, "But—"

"But of course we must defeat Boney first," I agreed.

"Perhaps Nick can get you that award of merit you've been hankering for, Marion" was Ronald's next inspiration.

I didn't want to give my new fiancé too much to contend with at one time. Sharing his title would do for the present. I never thought to be the Marchioness of anything.

"What order of merit?" Nick asked.

"It was just an idea of Tom Moore's," I assured him. "And now, if you gentlemen will excuse me, I shall retire. Aurelia will be accepting a proposal of marriage in the near future. I have a few notes I wish to jot down while they're fresh in my memory."

"You told him!" Ronald exclaimed.

"He guessed."

Nick picked up his hat. "I'll go with you. You might have forgotten a few details."

"No, they're indelibly etched in my memory. Every word. Belvoir admitting he cannot live without her . . ."

"I am beginning to wonder if he will be able to live with her!" he riposted, and followed me to my room, to add a few interesting, but I fear unprintable, bits to the proposal of Aurelia.